"What exactly are you trying to say to me?"

Tiago sighed, as if Lillie was being dense. And he hated himself for that, too, when she stiffened. "This cannot be an affair, Lillie. No matter what happened between us in Spain. Do you not understand? I will have to marry you."

Her eyes went wide. Her face paled, and not, his ego couldn't help but note, in the transformative joy a man in his position might have expected to see after a proposal. "Marry me? Marry *you*? Are you mad? On the strength of one night?"

"On the strength of your pregnancy. Because the Villela heir must be legitimate." He looked at her as if he had never seen her before and would never see her again, or maybe it was simply that he did not wish to say the thing he knew he must. But that was life, was it not? Forever forcing himself to do what was necessary, what was right. Never what he wanted. So he took a deep breath. "We will marry. Quickly. And once that happens, I will never touch you again."

USA TODAY bestselling, RITA® Award–nominated and critically acclaimed author **Caitlin Crews** has written more than one hundred and thirty books and counting. She has a master's and PhD in English literature, thinks everyone should read more category romance and is always available to discuss her beloved alpha heroes—just ask. She lives in the Pacific Northwest with her comic book–artist husband, is always planning her next trip and will never, ever read all the books in her to-be-read pile. Thank goodness.

Books by Caitlin Crews

Harlequin Presents

Willed to Wed Him
A Secret Heir to Secure His Throne
What Her Sicilian Husband Desires

Innocent Stolen Brides

The Desert King's Kidnapped Virgin
The Spaniard's Last-Minute Wife

The Outrageous Accardi Brothers

The Christmas He Claimed the Secretary
The Accidental Accardi Heir

Visit the Author Profile page
at Harlequin.com for more titles.

Caitlin Crews

A BILLION-DOLLAR HEIR
FOR CHRISTMAS

HARLEQUIN
PRESENTS

Recycling programs
for this product may
not exist in your area.

ISBN-13: 978-1-335-59303-0

A Billion-Dollar Heir for Christmas

Copyright © 2023 by Caitlin Crews

Harlequin Enterprises ULC
22 Adelaide St. West, 41st Floor
Toronto, Ontario M5H 4E3, Canada
www.Harlequin.com

Printed in U.S.A.

A BILLION-DOLLAR HEIR FOR CHRISTMAS

CHAPTER ONE

LILLIE MERTON ALMOST missed the fateful newscast entirely.

She'd been faffing about in the kitchen of the shared house she'd lived in since university, washing the usual mess of dishes left in the sink no matter how many times she asked her housemates to tidy up after themselves, cleaning the surfaces because no one else could manage it—apparently—and fixing herself a bit of beans on toast as if that might take away the deep chill of a November in Aberdeen, Scotland. And once her meal was ready, she hadn't intended to go and eat it in the shared lounge, because the reality was that she hadn't been the least bit comfortable with her housemates since her pregnancy had started to show.

There had been house meetings without her and then house meetings with her, but in the end, everyone had agreed. Regretfully, or so they claimed, but the house was comprised of merry singletons.

They were all much younger than Lillie, who had moved in here with her best mates from uni and had watched each and every one of them move out again as the years passed. To better jobs elsewhere, partners, marriages, madcap adventures abroad, and so on. Only Lillie remained, the decrepit thirty-year-old spinster who the newer housemates increasingly viewed as the de facto house mother.

Or had done until it was clear she was *actually* going to be a mother.

It was decided that the house was for young professionals who worked hard by day and liked a bit of a laugh by night. It was certainly no place for a baby. That was the verdict that had been delivered to her at the last house meeting with great solemnity, as if Lillie hadn't personally accepted each and every one of them into the house in the first place since hers was the name that had been on the lease the longest.

It wasn't as if she'd imagined she'd stay here in a house share with a wee bairn, thank you very much. She had as little desire to bung a cot and a changing table into her tiny bedroom as they did for her to parade an infant about through one of their Friday night drinking sessions before they went out to the city center bars and clubs. The same drinking sessions she always ended up cleaning up after even though *she* hadn't drunk herself legless in ages.

But no one liked to be *told* to leave, did they? Much less given an eviction date, and not very subtle threats that she would be chucked out if she didn't vacate on time—mostly because the ringleader of the younger set was dead set on having *her* best mate move in at the new year.

Needless to say, relationships had cooled all around.

Lillie was no longer cooking family-style meals for the lot of them or providing endless cups of tea and a sympathetic ear as needed. She rather thought they all regretted it. She'd seen more than one of the housemates mooning about, making big eyes in her direction while she—by far the best cook in the house, not that it was a distinction to be unduly proud of with this lot—made herself food for one and left them to their ready meals and boil-in-the-bag curries.

True, she was lonelier than she cared to admit, but at least she knew it was only going to be that way for a few more months. Then she would have a child to care for. She liked to tell herself living in this house with all these grown children was excellent preparation.

But that didn't make sitting in her bedroom and worrying over her fast-approaching future feel any better.

She didn't know why she stopped in the door of the lounge with her plate in hand, all that being the case. She *meant* to go straight on back to her room while it was still hers and settle in to watch videos on her mobile, while having a bit of the usual fret about her options.

Because she had options. It was just that Lillie wasn't sure she could face moving home with her parents in their quiet village. Lovely as they were, it had always been hard to live in the shadow of their grand, life-long love story—and she expected it would be doubly hard now that she'd gone and made it clear *she* would not be enjoying the same great passion as a single mum. She knew there was an extra room with her name on it in her cousin's place down in Glasgow, but she was trying to get her head around what it might be like not only to live with her very particular cousin Catriona, but what her child's life would be like under such a regime. In Glasgow, which was, according to everyone, including Lillie, far more metropolitan than home. Catriona called weekly to remind her the room was on offer, with babysitting on tap, and Lillie had always adored her persnickety cousin. That wasn't the issue. The issue was that this wasn't quite how Lillie had seen her life going.

Shouldn't have gone and gotten yourself up the duff then, auld lassie, she told herself stoutly.

And by that point she'd accidentally roamed far enough into the lounge that she could see the news program playing on the telly. Her housemate Martin fancied himself a man of the world when he was all of two and twenty, and his primary way of showing this was watching a bit of news every evening when no one else bothered.

Maybe later she would think about the series of tiny events and happenstance that led her to be standing there—beans and toast in hand, a little bit flushed of cheek from both the heat of the kitchen and her own enduring indignation at her ungrateful housemates—at the precise right moment to see the next segment as it began. A little bit of chatter from the anchor, and then there he was.

And even though he was on the screen of the communal telly in the same old house in Aberdeen where Lillie had lived for some eight years now, not even in person, it was the same as it had been five months ago in Spain.

She felt…transfixed. Rooted straight to the spot, but not by concrete or the like. It was as if electricity coursed through her, connecting her to the ground below, the sky above, and yet centering like one ongoing lightning strike inside her.

Lillie forgot to breathe. She forgot to do anything at all but stare—though at least this time he wasn't watching her do it.

There was only fresh-faced Martin as witness, turning around from his place on the sofa to frown at her.

"Why are you lurking about?" he asked crossly, because he had always been fond of Lillie and was covering his embarrassment at her visible pregnancy with bluster. It didn't help that she knew *why*. It was still a lot of blustering. "You know it does my head in to have people stood about behind me."

As if the path from the front hall to the kitchen wasn't directly behind the sofa he liked to sit in.

"Wouldn't want to do your head in, Martin," Lillie had the presence of mind to reply, dryly enough so that she felt slightly less despairing of herself when she turned and left the room with no explanation.

She had no memory of moving through the house, hefting her pregnant bulk up the narrow stairs to her room and then locking herself in. So that she could stand there, back to the door, for far too long. Panting less from the exertion than her emotional response to *seeing him* after all this time.

When she had given up on the notion that she might ever see him again.

And then, plunking her little plate down on her desk and then forgetting all about it, she snatched up her mobile to look up the name she'd seen flashed across the screen.

Tiago Villela.

She might have stopped to think. She might have paused to *breathe*, even, but she didn't have that option because typing his name auto-populated her screen without her even having to hit the search button.

It was like her *bones* shifted inside her. And everything else along with them.

Her eyes had not been deceiving her, there in the lounge.

It was him. It was really and truly *him*.

And he was not, as she'd come to tell herself over time, a pool boy who'd wandered into that particular part of the resort and found her there by the pool bar. Credulous and overwhelmed enough at a glance to take him at face value when he'd said there was no need to exchange anything more than the attraction they both felt so keenly.

She had tried to get the resort to help her once she'd faced the truth about the odd stomach issues and malaise she'd been battling as summer turned to fall, but all she could tell them was that he was dark and tall, almost supernaturally compelling, and had swept her off her feet.

"I am afraid you have described approximately ninety-seven percent of the gentlemen in Spain, madam," the resort's front desk had replied at last. Sniffily.

They had even gone back to her room, not his, so she didn't even have any potential context clues to go on. She'd had to face the fact that she possessed no possible way of identifying him, much less dutifully informing him that he was the father of the baby she was carrying.

He'd been gone before she'd woken up that next morning and Lillie might not have done anything like that before in her life, but she'd told herself she was delighted that he wasn't there for any awkward conversations that might make him seem as human as anyone. That way it had felt as if he was simply part and parcel of the Spanish adventure she'd never expected to have. She'd assured herself that she was *thrilled* that it was her happy little secret to keep.

She'd intended to keep it forever. Hoard it and hide it away, so she could enjoy all those blazing hot memories in the cold of Scotland that waited for her.

Alas.

Five months ago, she'd been set to have her usual chilly summer holiday. She normally spent a few days with her parents, wishing she could find that kind of love and life's purpose, then visited Catriona in Glasgow for a taste of the high life for a day or two. But as she'd been beginning to make her actual plans instead of daydreaming about, say, a flash holiday to New York City or the like that she would never *really* do, her longtime supervisor, the sleek and ferocious Patricia, had called her in all of a sudden one Tuesday morning.

Lillie had obviously assumed she was being summarily sacked.

Instead, Patricia had informed her that the company retreat had been moved at the last minute and Patricia had sadly already booked a week's holiday in Spain for the very same span of days. Lillie had then assumed that she'd be sent down to the dreary so-called retreat in Swindon in her boss's place because she couldn't imagine Patricia—shaped like a gazelle's front leg and sporting that jet black, always perfectly sleek hair—going without one of her precious weeks in the sun. Because Lillie had been Patricia's assistant for going on four years now and she'd shown up in her place before, if not at the same high executive level.

But that day Patricia had sighed and said that, sadly, her actual presence was required at Swindon and her assistant would not be able to fill in for her. She'd asked. What she wondered, she'd said then, was if Lillie might like to take her place in the pre-booked accommodation that Patricia would simply lose if she didn't use it?

"I would love to," Lillie had said frankly, "but I can't possibly pay for it."

Patricia had smiled in her usual way, a bit of a quirk of a closed mouth, nothing more. Her head had inclined slightly.

"You can consider it a bonus for your dedication these last years," she said. "One of us might as well have fun."

In the months since, Lillie had wondered what her boss's life—so seemingly glamorous from the outside—was actually like if her assistant was the only one she could think of to offer such a gift. Then again, the friends she knew of that Patricia had were as sharp and brittle as she was. She could see all too easily how Patricia might not wish to offer any of the lot of them any kind of gift of all.

For her part, Lillie didn't need to be asked twice. That was how she found herself in a flash resort in Spain for the most outrageous week of her life.

She hadn't *meant* to assume Patricia's identity. It was only that when she'd checked in, the staff had made that mistake and she hadn't corrected them. And then it had seemed as if pretending to be Patricia made everything that much more magical. Because while Lillie might not have gone ahead and taken part in the various activities offered of her own volition, she reckoned Patricia certainly would have.

So she did.

There were daytime excursions to Spanish sites, pools to visit, and boats to set sail on. There was dancing with strangers beneath the stars. There were yoga classes and massages, and Lillie indulged in them all. Because she was certain Patricia would have if she'd been there.

That was how she found herself slinking about in a bikini and a sarong on her last night there, as if she was the sort of person who wore such things, with her usually wild and unmanageable curly hair in a state of epic disarray that she'd decided was *a statement*. It had been one final and glorious evening in paradise. She'd gone to a cocktail hour gathering at the adults-only resort's prettiest poolside bar, so she could sip on the resort sangria that had helped keep her delightfully happy the whole week through.

One last night of glory, she'd told herself.

And that was where she'd met him.

Tiago Villela, who hadn't given her his name.

She stopped this little trip down memory lane, thanks to all the pictures of him on her mobile screen, because she needed a bit of reminding that she was still there in her same old bedroom in the same shared house in Aberdeen. Not in Spain again. Not sunburnt everywhere with freckles she'd never seen in the weak Scottish sun, her hair a mess of snarls and salt, more drunk on the sea air and soft breezes than the all-inclusive drinks.

Lillie wasn't surprised to find herself breathing a bit too quickly, her head going a little funny. That was how she'd felt then, too.

She went and sank down on her bed. And because she was alone, locked away from prying eyes and not required to make the best of anything, she let the full scope of the emotions that buffeted her take hold.

Because she'd pretended all this time that it had all been a bit of fun. Once she'd gotten the test results and had fully accepted that they were real, she'd understood at once that she would be keeping the baby. She had never considered any other path.

People would think whatever they would think, she'd told herself. And mostly it turned out that they thought she was seizing the only chance she'd ever have to be a mother—which was insulting—but then, so was the clear speculation on the part of every person she knew that she might have ditched the Spanish holiday altogether and got herself a turkey baster baby at a clinic. So impossible was it, her meanest housemate informed her, to imagine Lillie actually naked and having it off with a man.

"You're not really the sort, are you?" she'd asked pityingly, as if Lillie was making up stories. "It's horrible to think of it."

"Then perhaps don't strain yourself thinking about it," Lillie had replied, half laughing at the *affront* of it all from this girl whose hair she'd held back while she was sick after too many Saturday nights out to count. "If it's so *horrible*. Heaven forfend."

But she alone knew that her desire to be a mother had nothing to do with the spinsterhood that seemed top of mind to all and sundry. It was that it was *his* baby.

That they had made the child together on the most magical night of Lillie's life.

And once she understood that there would be no locating him, as if he been some kind of phantom she'd made up as the last, best part of her Spanish daydream, the baby she carried became that much more precious to her.

Because it was all she had left of him. All she would ever have.

She hoarded the truth to her like the treasure it was.

What did it matter to her if everyone thought she'd gone and got paralytic one night abroad to end up this way? Or that she'd forgone the notion of finding a man entirely and had visited a doctor's office to get herself pregnant, something her younger housemates clearly thought was shameful. She knew better.

Oh, how she knew better.

And when she was alone, she liked to go over the facts of that night. One moment after the next, committing each and every one of them to memory. Because every single second she'd spent with that man was like spun gold, each moment its own bright coin, and all of it was hers now to do with what she liked.

Mine, she thought, with a protective hand over her swollen belly.

"Mine and yours," she said out loud to the bairn within, because this was where she could be honest about Spain. Here in the safety of her room, though, she'd be giving even that up soon for the false smiles and forced laughter about her supposed behavior at her parents' or her cousin's.

Though she knew she was lucky to have choices, and hated neither one of them, she still wanted to hold on to *these* moments as long as she could. When it was just her and her memories and the baby they'd made tucked up safe and sound inside her. Healthy as could be, according to the doctor.

The truth was, Lillie had never made it to the bar

that night because the moment she'd laid eyes on *him*, alcohol would have been superfluous at best.

He had been far more intoxicating, even at a glance.

And this was the truth that she could never tell a soul. Because no one would believe her. They would think her a sad cow, at best. They would imagine she was telling tales to preserve her pride, or some such thing. She could see it in her mind's eye, the way they would pity her. And it wasn't that she would have minded that too much, really, because she wasn't so dim that she didn't realize that far too many people in her life already pitied her.

It was more that what had happened that night felt sacred.

Because it was as simple and as complicated as this: she had looked up, and he had been there before her. There had been one split second before he saw her, when she had very nearly formed the dazed sort of thought that he was *astonishing*—

That rumpled, too-long dark hair. Those eyes, not green and yet not blue, like a sea too pretty to name. That *face* of his, an angel gone dark, with the fierce blade of a nose like some kind of ancient gladiator, God help her—

But then he had clapped his startled gaze to hers and it was as if everything that followed had been inevitable.

More than that, *magical*.

Lillie could no more have stopped it than she could flown over the moon with her own two arms as wings, and anyway, she didn't regret a bit of it.

She'd almost rather that everyone she knew dismissed the whole thing as a drunken shag with some stranger, as tawdry and shameful and uncharacteristic as they could imagine. Better that than attempt to explain to them the unvarnished truth.

The weight of what had flared there between them had been almost too much to bear.

It still felt like that now.

Too much.

Too big.

Too intense.

It had exploded in that single glance, so suddenly, that she knew without a shred of doubt that both of their lives had changed forever in that moment. And more, that both of them had known that, right then, in the same flashing instant.

As if the world was divided into *before* and *after*.

Here in her bedroom, she replayed it in her mind the way she always did, as if it were new. As if it were happening all over again.

"Who are you?" he'd demanded, coming to her side and looking at her with an impassioned sort of *vividness* that had shaken her. She could feel it inside her now, as much a part of her as her own blood. Even then, when it was new, it had felt *right*. That he should frown down at her as if she was an apparition. As if he had found something he hadn't known he had been searching for. And as he came to stand before her, his closeness had felt like a gift.

Because he was there at last and though she had only seen him for the first time a moment ago, she felt as if he was still not close enough when she had waited *forever* for him.

"Who are *you*?" she had asked in return.

But neither one of them had answered that question.

They'd stood there, frozen in place, while people moved all around them. They stood there, rapt and amazed, breathing the same air that smelled of flowers and sweet salt.

Together at last, Lillie had thought, though that made no sense.

Lillie had known even then that she would never be able to explain the thing that bloomed between them, that feeling that her whole life had led her to this moment where they finally clapped eyes on each other. As if it had all been preordained. As if they'd been born for this, to find each other and hold on tight.

If she'd been swept up by the breeze itself and lost high above in the Spanish skies, forever, she would not have been at all surprised.

And in a way, that was precisely what had happened.

They didn't speak. They didn't laugh and get to know each other, flirt and dance and take part in the usual rituals of such evenings, according to every book she'd ever read and television show she'd ever watched. All of that would have made sense.

But nothing about that man made any sense.

It had been as if they had both been struck by the same lightning and had to stand there at the side of the pool in that resort, staring at each other in wonder, fascination, and a kind of panic, as they each tried to make sense of the way they burned.

Lillie could have stood there for lifetimes on end. It was possible she did, but didn't notice, because all she could see was him.

Until finally he had reached over, as if he did not quite trust his own hand, and had fit it gently to her cheek.

And then they'd both made the same sort of sound, a kind of sharp inhalation, and yet another bolt of that same electricity had shot through them both.

"I think," he said quietly, that voice of his dark and deep and tinged with flavors she could not identify, "we should take this somewhere private, *benzinho*. Yes?"

"Yes," Lillie had breathed.

And she had said that again and again and again that night. *Yes.*

Yes, yes, yes.

And now, lying on her bed, she felt a great sob work its way through her, though it wasn't quite grief. Or a darker sort of joy. It wasn't even sorrow. It was all of those things and none of them, because she knew his name now.

She knew his name.

The next day at work, she put together the latest presentation so that Patricia could take charge of her noon meeting with her usual ferocious competence that made the men she managed call her *the dragon lady*, not quite behind her back.

And while Patricia held court in the boardroom, Lillie did a bit of a deep dive on Tiago Villela.

Last night it had been enough to look at pictures of him, confirm that she had not been drunk on sangria, and get a general sense of the man. That he was no pool boy. He was powerful. He was enormously, almost absurdly wealthy. She had believed those things on the night, but as time passed and he had been unidentifiable, she'd tried to convince herself that she'd made it all up.

If anything, she had underestimated exactly how wealthy and powerful he really was.

But she wasn't interested in his net worth. She was far more interested in his location.

Because, she told herself piously, he deserved to know that he had a child on the way.

It had nothing at all to do with the fact that she wanted—desperately—to see him again.

Or so she tried to convince herself as she sat at her desk, pretending to be thinking only of her unborn child.

It took a little digging and a few carefully placed phone calls, once again pretending to be people she was not—namely, the secretary of a specific, higher-placed woman in her organization, because she doubted very much that a man like Tiago Villela could be found by anyone socially if he didn't wish it.

And that was how, in the space of an hour and a half, she discovered not only that Tiago Villela was currently at his London headquarters but that he would remain there for the remainder of the week.

Once she knew that, it wasn't terribly hard to ring down to London and manage to set an informational meeting with him—and the woman she was not—to take place the following afternoon. Because Tiago Villela was apparently well known for taking meetings that would normally go to his underlings. He liked to hear some cold calls and pitches himself—but only on select Wednesday afternoons when he was in the office and had no raging fires to put out elsewhere. That had been the point of the news segment on him. His surprising *accessibility*.

And once she'd secured the meeting, she found herself looking, almost regretfully, for the next cheap flight south because the sleeper train would take far too long.

"I beg your pardon?" Patricia asked in astonishment when Lillie informed her of this upon her return from the meeting. "You're leaving in the morning? Are you mad?"

"Not *mad* as such," Lillie replied. "Though I am pregnant."

And maybe there was something wrong with her that she found it amusing, the way Patricia let her gaze travel down the length of her body to her bump, then back up.

"I just thought you'd gotten fat," Patricia said, with her usual directness that Lillie had come to find refreshing. It was such a pleasant change from her housemates' typical passive-aggressiveness.

"I have," Lillie agreed, tapping her round belly with a laugh. "But not from too many sweets, I'm afraid." But there was no time to laugh. She had a plane to catch in the morning.

Because it was the right thing to do, as she kept telling herself. That was all.

"I finally tracked down the father, you see. And this is my chance to let him know. So he can be involved in his child's life, if he wishes."

Patricia had eyed her for a moment, looking almost wise—and far kinder than usual. It put a lump in Lillie's throat.

"I certainly hope he's someone you can stomach having in your life, then," Patricia said, almost gently. "And the child's life, for that matter. I've personally never met a man who would be worth the bother. You could also...not trouble yourself with a bloke at all, surely? In this day and age?"

"It's the right thing to do," Lillie said.

Virtuously.

Patricia only looked at her, for a moment that stretched on far too long. "Right. Well. Better you than me, my girl."

Lillie thought about that a lot as she boarded the plane, with only a measly carry-on bag she still had to pay extra for. She thought about that when she landed in Heathrow Airport, heaving with people, and had to work out how to get herself where she needed to go on the legendary Tube.

It was all a bit much for someone who had taken precisely one school trip to London, long ago.

She turned it all this way and that inside of her, the way she'd been doing for months, as she walked down gray, cold streets and got turned around, then had to retrace her steps. And when she finally reached the right building and went inside, it wasn't much better.

Because this was a different sort of before-and-after moment, she knew. She explained to the security guards that she had been sent to step into a meeting for her boss at the last moment, showed her work identification, and was directed to the gold-edged lift that offered only one stop—the very top floor.

As the elevator rose, taking her closer and closer to a lightning strike once again—or, maybe, no lightning at all, and she could admit she wasn't sure how she'd handle *that* if it happened—she slid her hand down over her belly, held on tight, and tried to get her pulse to settle.

"I think this is the best thing," she said aloud, and pretended she was talking to the baby inside her instead of to herself. "I really do. It's the right thing to do no matter what happens now."

And when the lift doors slid open, she walked out into a marble lobby and felt nothing short of dizzy at all the understated—and not so understated— opulence.

It took every scrap of willpower she had not to turn around and leg it back to Aberdeen as fast as she could. She didn't belong here. She didn't know what to do with all this obvious wealth beaming down from chandeliers better suited to castles, by her reckoning, marble for miles, and everything gilt-edged and gleaming.

But she was to be a mother soon enough and so it didn't matter if she, personally, was brave. She couldn't let that matter. What mattered was what she did to make her child think he or she could be, too, and it started here.

So she took a deep breath, fixed a smile on her face as she announced herself to reception, and prepared herself for another lightning storm.

One way or another.

CHAPTER TWO

WHEN HIS OFFICE door opened, Tiago Villela glanced up from a typical afternoon of paperwork between meetings and froze.

"Impossible," he bit out.

He was rising, then, without thought. His gaze was fixed on the face of the woman who stood just inside his office, as if she was a ghost.

Was she a ghost?

But her eyes were too big and too blue, just as he remembered. Just as he'd replayed in his head so many times since. He had seen them hot with need and bright with laughter, but he knew them even now, far more cool and solemn, and yet too filled with life to be anything like *spectral*.

He would know her face anywhere. A narrow oval, no longer bright with too much sun or sprinkled with freckles on either side of her nose, each and every one of which he had tasted and committed to memory. Today she looked pale, and paler still as she stood there and regarded him with such determination. But most of all, he recognized that hair. Her riot of dark blond and brown spirals was far more subdued today than he remembered them, but still clearly *hers*. For he could still feel the soft coils against his palms, having held her tight with his fingers sunk deep in her curls while he'd driven into her again and again and again—

God, the ways this woman had *haunted* him, ghost or memory, did not bear thinking of in the light of day.

"Your name is not Patricia MacDonald," he grated out. "Your room was in her name."

And he was Tiago Villela. He had inherited fortunes from both sides of his family and made his own to match. His name was whispered in corridors of power and invoked in corporate boardrooms from London to Hong Kong, then back again. He had no need to waste his talents playing games like poker, no matter how sweet the pot—not when there were corporate negotiations with far higher stakes that he could win.

And did.

All that and yet he—praised far and wide as a man who might as well have been a glacier, with whole winters running through his veins—had given away his obsession with this woman without even being prompted.

He expected her to look triumphant, as people

in his world so rarely did in his presence, but she floored him by smiling instead.

As if he was still deep inside her.

"At least you had a name to go on," she replied, and it was that voice again. *Her* voice. Slightly husky and shaping words in a way that sounded like music to his ears. That same voice that seemed equal parts sex and laughter, like a punch in the gut. And a much harder sucker punch lower still. "I thought you were the pool boy."

Tiago was certain that every member back down along his ancestral lines, Spanish and Portuguese alike, had a bit of a communal roll in their assorted mausoleums at that.

But he couldn't seem to muster up the appropriate level of outrage.

Not when he could feel his heartbeat inside his chest like it was fighting to get out and more, had a decent chance of winning. The whole of his body had gone taut and wild, as if he was still in that appalling hotel in the part of Spain he usually tried to avoid— overrun as it was by entirely too many tourists— after concluding a wholly unsatisfactory business meeting. He could still remember it entirely too well. One moment he had been annoyed beyond reason at the waste of his time and the next he'd been captivated by her face. That impossibly compelling *face* that he had spent a great deal of energy since convincing himself could not possibly have been real.

Because he had not been able to find her, and that was an unacceptable outcome, so it had been much preferable to imagine he'd perhaps allowed himself to be overserved in the hotel bar that night. He, who never allowed that kind of loss of control. He, who had never had trouble maintaining a grip on reality in all his days.

Still. These were the things he had attempted to convince himself, and staring at her now, *right here in his office*, he understood why.

If anything, she was even more compelling than he'd allowed himself to recall.

"I looked for you," he told her, his voice darker now. Almost as if he was straying into the realms of temper, when he did not typically allow himself such indulgences. It was that *face* of hers. He could not imagine how she lived a whole life somewhere, walking around just…*looking* like that, without a warning label. It was unconscionable. "It was apparent at once that you did not use your own name."

"You can't have looked too hard, then, can you," she replied, cheerfully enough, as if that changed the fact that she was insulting him. "Since I work with the real Patricia MacDonald. It was her holiday, you see. She pre-booked. And who was I to argue when everyone kept calling me by her name?"

"I looked for you," he said again, and this time it felt like a relief to feel the stirring of what he assumed was temper, somewhere deep within him.

Because that felt right in these unprecedented circumstances. It felt more like him, at any rate. Because he was not a man who ever *felt* much of anything around women. They came and went like hours in the day, and he thought as much of them when they were gone.

For his had always been a life of duty and accomplishments, not dissolution and selfishness. The Villelas were not raised to rest on their laurels. No idle sons of wealth cluttered up *his* family tree. While there might have been a questionable cousin or status-obsessed great-uncle on his mother's more easygoing side, the Villelas had produced generation upon generation of heirs who knew full well that their role upon this planet was to act as steward of what had come before as well as the legacy and nobility of the Villela name. And more, that the power that name wielded should only and ever be used for good.

It was true that some of his forebears had looked for some wiggle room in that last directive, but Tiago wasn't one of them. He had always taken his responsibilities seriously.

And in all that time, this woman was the only thing that had ever worked its way beneath his skin, like a sharp bit of wood that wouldn't come out. He had not forgotten her. He had not spent a single night since meeting her without wondering where she was.

She had made him do things he would have sworn he would never, ever do, or even conceive of doing—

like send one of his men to a dreary oil-industry-adjacent conference in Swindon to intercept a woman who didn't exist.

"Right name, wrong face," he'd growled when they'd sent him a shot of the wrong woman.

And had not liked how difficult that was for him to accept when he had not exactly furnished her with his contact details that night.

He realized that he was staring at her—at that impossible face of hers that he had imagined, and taken apart, and imagined anew too many times to count in the months since the night they'd shared.

"How did you find me?" he asked in the same dark manner, because she didn't need to know anything about what had happened since that night. Only that they hadn't exchanged names. But as she looked back at him, he knew the answer. "That news program."

He said it with something near enough to disgust, though that wasn't his prevailing feeling in this moment. It was only that this was too unsettling, after so long. It was too much. He had too many memories as it was and he didn't want them.

Or maybe it was that he had given up on this particular wish and yet here it was, granted all the same.

It made him feel…unsteady.

And Tiago was a Villela. He was made to be a mountain, as solid as sheer rock with high, proud peaks. He was bright with impassable snow.

He was not *unsteady*.

And yet.

"The news, yes," she agreed. And was that the faintest hint of color on her cheeks? "I caught the program quite by accident."

"But I am meant to be meeting with a representative of…" He trailed off, because he hadn't committed the name to memory. He would now, however, assuming… "Is that your real name? Whatever name you used to make this appointment?"

Her cheeks took on a bit more color. "Julieta Braithwaite really is a vice president in the company, but I'm not her."

"So these are more games. You hunted me down off a news program to turn up and continue the pretense." Tiago reminded himself that despite the night they'd shared and the fact that it had felt more like a reunion than a first meeting, he didn't know this woman at all. Why should he think less of her for these games? Why should he have any opinion about her at all? Still, he kept going. "Why?"

And for the first time, either that night or today, he thought she looked uneasy. "That's a bit of delicate matter."

It was only then, as her hands went to the wide collar of the great, shawl-like thing she wore as a coat, that he actually stopped staring at the face that had haunted his fondest dreams for so long. And took a look at the rest of her.

Even before she'd finished opening up her coat, he could see that there were changes in her body. Her breasts were so full now he felt certain they would overflow his large palms. And below, the soft belly he recalled so perfectly looked hard, high, and round.

Very much as if she was…

He became aware of harsh breathing, but he could not tell if it was hers or his. Letting his eyes move over the clear evidence he could see before him, it was clear that his mind wished to reject what he saw. To assert that he could not have been so reckless. To tell himself that he must have made certain this could not occur.

But she was wearing a soft dress that clung to her body as he had, once, and there could be no mistaking it.

The woman was pregnant.

The repercussions of that seemed to fall through him like all that hard, snow-covered stone he had only just been thinking about.

"Right," she said with forced brightness. "I see you've guessed my happy news. Well. I was prepared to make a go of it on my own. I think that's important for you to know. But I also thought that it was the moral thing to inform the father either way. I called the hotel and tried to give them some sort of description that would lead to your name, but they couldn't help me."

"I was not a guest of the hotel," he said, prosaically. "I was there for a meeting."

Because nothing at all made sense, and he could only keep staring. As if waiting to laugh at whatever joke this was that she was pulling here, even though something in him knew full well that was not likely to happen.

"Ah," was all she said.

And he was aware of her in that same overwhelming, impossible way he had been in Spain. He could see her pulse beat in her throat. He could see how each breath she took made her breasts move. In the whole of his life, he had never found a woman ripe with child to be anything but an object of distant interest, unrelated to him in any way, but this woman was something else. He could feel his sex stir as he looked at her. At all that *roundness*. At the changes her body had undergone already. Everything about her fascinated him and made his hands itch to discover how each and every bit of newness stood up to his memories.

As if she was his when she was not.

When he did not want any woman to be *his*, not like that, with all that need and longing and the sort of mad passion that ruined men entirely.

"I was weighing up my options," she told him, speaking into that loud, ringing silence between them. "But I really do think the best course of action is to take the spare room in my cousin's flat in

Glasgow. She likes bit of company, mine in particular, though she can be a fussy, *fykie* sort. And she's quite committed to staying single as well, so between the two of us I reckon we can make our own family." She swallowed, as if this was hard for her when it didn't sound as if it was. Just as she had that night, she talked to him as if he was a regular man. As if they were already in the middle of a conversation and could pick it up and put it down as they chose. But he did not wish to be charmed by her. Not now. "Still, when I saw you on the telly I knew that regardless of any plans I might or might not have made, I had to do the right thing."

He moved closer then, and though what he longed to do was run his hands over that tempting bump of hers, he refrained. That felt too intimate. As if it would be straying too far into the realm of something he couldn't take back. Some terrible longing he did not wish to face.

As if this mattered in ways he did not wish to acknowledge. Already.

Still, something in him corrected.

He ignored it, reaching over and taking her chin in his hand. And he could feel the sharp little breath she took, as if she could feel that touch the same way he did. All of that instant heat, like a flash that illuminated them both.

"Your name," he commanded her, in a voice that sounded nothing at all like his. "Tell me your name."

"Lillie," she whispered back, her eyes like the sky in the lands he was from and nearly as wide. "Lillie Elizabeth Merton. Lately of Aberdeen, Scotland."

Many things surged in him then. Memories of that night when Tiago had acted so unlike himself that it had haunted him ever since.

Though he could admit, now, that he had also allowed himself a measure of relief that it really had been as if he'd created her in his own mind. As if he'd dreamed the whole thing, after all.

Only now did he understand what a gift that had been.

Because he had no place in his life for this. For *her.* For that unquenchable fire that had swept over both of them on that poolside terrace in Spain and had been firing sparks at him from his own, treacherous memory ever since.

He made himself let go of her chin, because the touch of her skin radiated through him, making him question everything he'd ever thought about what he would and would not accept. Who he would and would not allow himself to become.

What he was even capable of feeling.

"Lillie," he said, as if tasting the name.

And he set aside all of the things he should have told her then. About who he was. About what his family had always expected of him. What the weight of his legacy meant and what he did to manage it.

These things that could not change, that would

not change as long as he lived, and yet all he could seem to do was repeat her name.

Like some kind of prayer of deliverance.

When he knew better.

Villelas cannot be men of passion, his quietly stern father had told him many years ago. *It is not who we are. It is not what is expected of us. We must hold ourselves to a higher level. We must exhort ourselves to become a credit to our bloodline. Your mother is my bride because her family is like ours and thus she understands the traditions that shape and guide us. Because of this basic understanding, there is nothing in our relationship that could ever threaten our dual legacy. Do you understand?*

Tiago had not been raised to entertain the sort of feelings that felled so many of his peers. The only person he had ever loved, and who had loved him back, was the grandmother he'd lost when he was young—and he had quickly learned what a liability that was. What a terrible carnage grief was, on the inside.

And so he comprehended what his father had been telling him all too well now.

Lust. Passion. Greed. These were things that led venal men to murder and great men to stumble, but he would not allow any of them to do such things to *him*. He had always handled his body's needs with women who understood there was nothing more to be had from him than the fleeting pleasure they shared.

He took pains to never, ever let greed dictate his decisions. He treated the power in his name like a kind of volatile poison that could kill him as easily as it could gain him anything, and there was only one night in his entire life he had ever risked any of it.

He would not do it again.

Tiago did not trouble himself with emotion, passion, or any of the things that made humans act so contrary to their own interests. He did not need to learn his lessons more than once.

He should not have required the reminder.

And so even though it felt a bit too little, too late, he stepped back then. He looked at Lillie for a long moment, then reached around her to open up his office door.

"Caroline, if you please," he said to his secretary in the next room, "have the plane waiting for me. And cancel the rest of my day."

That was unusual, but the unflappable Caroline had been with him for over a decade, and she did not so much as blink. "Right away, Mr. Villela."

"You could have sent a letter," he said to Lillie when he closed the door again, and he told himself it was only right that he let his gaze go cool and assessing. Not only was it right, but it also felt far more rational that he could trust himself to take one look at her without the whole world getting knocked back on its axis, for a change. "Instead, you chose to come in person. To my place of business, under an assumed name. In a pretty dress, no less."

She blinked, and looked down at her dress. "It seemed like the sort of thing people wear in giddy London." She ran her hands down the dress as if she'd only just seen it for the first time, then looked back at him, her eyes sparkling. "Is it not? I wouldn't want to seem a Scottish country mouse. Not while informing a man that he's the father of my baby. That would be a tragedy, I'm sure."

And he really, truly could have done without the reminder that she was this charming. That she alone seemed so capable of charming *him*, when no one else had ever seemed to possess the faintest shred of the ability.

"We are going to have to come to terms, you and I," he told her, channeling his father's deliberate sternness.

Her eyes did not dim, precisely. But she did hitch her chin up a notch or two, so in the end, perhaps it was the same thing. "I don't know what sort of terms you mean."

"There will have to be tests. I mean no disrespect, but I'm sure you understand that we must both be certain."

That time, there was no question that she looked dimmer, and it was shocking to him that he disliked it. Intensely. "Do you mean a paternity test?"

"*Benzinho*, you know who I am now," Tiago said.

Kindly, he thought. "You cannot imagine that a man in my position can simply take it on faith when told he is unexpectedly a father, can you?"

But he could see by her crestfallen expression that she had imagined exactly that. And he held back from letting himself get cold and cutting with her, as he knew he could. It would be easy enough to make it abundantly clear that he had earned every bit of his glacial reputation, but this woman was different.

Because as much as he wanted to imagine that she was a scheming, naive fool to come here and think he would simply believe her, he knew better. That long night they'd shared and the connection between them was something he still couldn't begin to puzzle out.

But he did not need to tell her that, either.

Tiago waited until her shoulders seemed to deflate, and then nodded. "I will call my personal physician from the car."

He thought she might argue then, but all she did was look at him as if he was coming into focus—but slowly—until he felt something in him lose its place.

A sensation he could not say he cared for in the least.

"Take all the tests you like," she said after a moment, her voice huskier than before. Quieter. "But I shouldn't like to miss my return flight to Aberdeen, if at all possible."

And Tiago had not become the man he was, in this position he enjoyed, by engaging in unnecessary arguments. Even before the tests came back, he had made up his mind.

He did not share that, either. He knew it made no sense, and that in all other areas he was seen as the soul of prudence and circumspection. The world was filled with scheming people, men and women alike, forever running their little cons to better their positions. To change their lives. To get a little more and leave others with a little less. He'd seen it all in his day—and there had always been various attempts to wrap him up in such webs, too. It came with the territory.

But he was not at all surprised when the paternity test came back with the indisputable proof he hadn't needed, because he already knew that he intended to keep her.

That was the troubling thing about Lillie.

If he'd had his way, even five months ago when he hadn't been looking for anything but a car to take him away from that loud, garish resort, he wouldn't have left her.

Lillie. Her name lilted inside him like a melody. It was both not at all the name he would have chosen for her and at the same time, perfect. Even the way she spelled it at the doctor's office—not quite a flower, but something else. Something *her*.

"I hope you are not too distressed by the news," she said in that arch, Scottish way of hers when they were back in his car and his driver was making his way through the typical snarls of London traffic.

He should have expected the question. He wasn't sure why he hadn't. "*Distressed* is not the word I would choose."

"This is slightly disappointing," Lillie confided in him, once more as if they were the best of casual friends. "I expected at least a few accusations of whoring myself about before the results came in. Some thundering on, at the least. You seem to be accepting this rather easily. I thought men in your tax bracket were forever ranting on about bloodlines and legacies and all the rest of it. *The shores of Pemberley polluted* and so on."

And he remembered this, too. That in places where other people, and specifically other woman, might cower—Lillie had done the opposite. She got very dry. And amused. And there was something about both of those things that he found entertaining, when he had been told a thousand times by business associates and romantic assignations alike that he was bereft of even the faintest nod toward any kind of sense of humor. Something he had always chosen to wear as a badge of honor, because he was a Villela. He had things of import to accomplish in this life. Laughter was the province of the weak. He couldn't recall ever seeing his father or mother do more than offer a genteel smile.

It was one more thing that was different with this woman.

Maybe it was in that moment that the decision he'd already made firmed into certainty.

"Until now you have perhaps not had a particularly good overview of my character, I think," he told her then. "As you imagined me some kind of pool boy Lothario, of all things. But I hope I have never been the sort of man to deny reality when it is right there before me."

She looked as if she wanted to say something to that, but didn't. Her blue eyes found his, then dropped, and he found himself transfixed by the way she moved her hands over the rounded swell of her belly.

Tiago had never wanted to touch anything as much as he wanted to touch her, then. It was as if wanting his hands on her was some kind of ache within him. And he was forced to face the fact that he was not used to wanting things he could not have. For all he liked to think of himself as a man who was somehow not out of touch with the real world, despite his wealth and power, perhaps he had been fooling himself about that all along.

But he remembered too well what it had been like to lie with this woman on that bed in Spain. To explore every part of her, and let her do the same in return, and lose himself somehow in a communion that should never have affected him the way that it did.

He had not felt out of touch that night. He had felt, for the first and only time in his life, not like a Villela at all—but like a man. A regular, red-blooded man, who wanted her.

Only her, in every possible way the two of them could imagine.

But he forced himself to thrust those memories aside.

He did not reach over and touch her, though the more he yearned to do it, the more stern he was forced to get with himself. Because the way forward was clear, as he had discovered long ago. It would require self-control on his part, but that had never been something he had struggled with before—self-control was how he'd survived his childhood after his grandmother had died. His self-control was the only part of him that his parents had ever praised, and therefore he had made certain he exerted it over all aspects of his life.

A bit of deprivation was good for a man's character. Tiago was living proof.

Surely all that was needed with Lillie was a bit of exposure therapy to weaken this hold she had on him, that was all. All he needed was to banish the ghost of her and focus on the real, live woman instead.

Because it was her memory that had haunted him. The reality of her would not—he knew this, because no real woman ever had.

And once he vanquished this *pull* she exerted on

him, he would be himself again. Perfectly capable of what was necessary.

That was what he wanted. Not those haunting memories that kept him up in the night, dreaming of things that could never be.

He did not touch her, but he turned so that he could face her, there in the back of the car. "It must have been difficult to get used to this notion that you are to become a mother, I imagine."

"There was a bit of denial at first," she agreed, with that astonishing frankness that he hadn't the slightest idea what to do with. "But I've come round."

He was not sure that he had ever seen anything quite as remarkable as this woman who he thought he'd lost forever smiling at him the way she did then, her hands folded gently over the mound of the child she carried.

His child.

His child.

But that, too, was neither here nor there.

"All I ask is that you allow me the chance to *come round* to it as well."

She inclined her head then, as if she was royalty. He should have found her gauche and presumptuous, he who had squired princesses on his arm. But he did not.

He really did not.

"You have a fair few more months," she said, her eyes gleaming. "I expect you'll catch up."

He wanted to laugh, but he was not that sort of man, so he frowned instead. The very soul of the exacting Villela code of conduct that his parents had modeled for him from the start. He was just as happy neither one of them was here now to see how he'd fallen short.

"I will need this time to get to know you as well, Lillie," he told her. Reprovingly. "As something more than a bit of pleasure." And he knew, when he saw the flash of emotion in her gaze, that she didn't like to call what had happened between them something so dismissive. And more, that he had called it that for precisely this reason. "For you are now the mother of the Villela heir, like it or not. And both of us will have to come to terms with that."

CHAPTER THREE

LILLIE HAD NEVER been to Portugal before.

But then, Lillie had never really been *anywhere* before, not really, aside from London that one time. She'd otherwise remained in Scotland for the most part, with only the occasional trip down to Whitby with her parents to spend a few cold summer beach days in that holiday caravan park they liked so well.

Her trip to Spain had been the start of a glorious new international *jet-set* kind of a life. That was what she'd told herself all the way home, still sunburnt and buzzing and half-wild from her night with Tiago. Spain was the *beginning*, she'd told herself as the plane landed in drizzly, bleak Aberdeen. The future was going to feel just as magic as that long, lush night had done.

She'd meant it. She really had. But thus far her glorious jet-setting had been confined to daydreams and bright, happy travel documentaries. Then she'd discovered she was pregnant and such things seemed even more out of reach than they'd been before. Because all it took was one positive pregnancy test to start thinking a lot more seriously about the reality of…well, everything. Such as the things she'd put off thinking about for ages, like why she was still living in a house better suited to new university graduates. Or what she really and truly wanted to do with her life, which she was pretty sure wasn't making PowerPoint presentations.

The trouble was, all of that felt like a fight and Lillie had never been much for fighting. That seemed part and parcel of the sort of passion her parents enjoyed, but had missed *her* little life entirely.

Sometimes she even told herself that a small, comfortable life was a virtue.

But nothing about this day was small or comfortable.

And Lillie was not at all prepared to be swept out of Tiago's car on a rainy, blustery tarmac somewhere outside of London, then ushered up the steps to the private jet that waited there like it was the most ordinary thing in the world when it certainly was no such thing.

It was all she could do not to gape about her like the overset, overawed country lass she most assuredly was.

And it had not been a long flight, but it had certainly been eye-opening.

Just like his office, the plane was a pageant of

gleaming marble mixed in with the liberal application of rich, dark woods and lashings of plush, inviting leather besides. There were *couches* littered about the place like it was a high-class lounge in the sort of desperately posh and unaffordable flats Lillie only looked at in magazines. And in case anyone was feeling peckish there was a full cream tea service with plate after plate of clever little sandwiches cut *just so*, airy crumpets with pots of butter and jam, and scones drowning in clotted cream that tasted of dreams come true.

Lillie had three, just to be certain.

It was all a far cry indeed from the tiny packet of overly dry pretzels she'd had to pay for on her desperately uncomfortable flights to and from Spain and down from Aberdeen this morning. Bargain airfare, after all, was about efficiency, not comfort.

Tiago's jet was nicer than any home Lillie had lived in.

It was nicer than any home she'd ever *been in*, for that matter.

Tiago had left her to her tea, retreating to what one of the stewards called "the office suite," to be distinguished from "the staterooms," to handle some of his business. Leaving Lillie to scoff scones and tea and darling little *petits fours* and reflect upon the fact that she hadn't objected when he'd suggested she not go back to Aberdeen at all.

"Not when there is so much to sort out between

the two of us," he had said in that way of his that made everything inside her feel light and shivery. Especially when he had looked at her bump, in a way she wanted to call almost…possessive. It had made her heart flip inside her chest. "Excuse me, I mean the three of us."

The man was a menace.

But apparently she didn't think he was *too much* of a menace, because there she was. Lounging about on an achingly lovely leather couch on a plane she reckoned was nicer than some of those old medieval castles with all the dungeons and drafts. Having a bit of a high tea all on her own while she was being flown off to sunny Portugal at a moment's notice, *thank you very much*.

She had texted Patricia, though she knew that was unlikely to make her boss happy.

It looks like this might take longer than expected. Not sure when I'll be back, to be honest.

The reply had been surprising.

You take as long as you need. And don't be afraid to hold his feet to the fire, either. Bloody men.

Lillie had wanted to send back something suitably rousing and woman powery in solidarity, but the truth of it was that no fires held to feet seemed to be necessary. She wasn't sure what to make of it. Her stomach had been in knots all the way to his office, certain that he would be horrible to her. Or that his battalions of staff would bar her from even laying eyes on him.

She'd expected a fight, was the thing, and this didn't seem like anything of the kind.

Though, somehow, she couldn't quite let herself be lulled into any sort of sense of security. Not quite yet.

They landed in Portugal some while later, the sea in the distance as they flew in over rolling vineyards and stretches of green that looked like golf courses. Lillie felt she ought to ask questions about where they were going, but she was much too sated and drowsy from the lovely tea she'd consumed. Added to the fact that her pregnancy made her a whole lot sleepier than she'd ever been before.

Still, she followed Tiago out into a glorious bit of sunshine happily enough, pleased and yet, now, unsurprised to see yet another vehicle waiting for them. No scrabbling about looking for Tube stations or taxis for Tiago Villela. The SUV that waited near the airfield looked suitably rugged, given that they were out in a bit of countryside, and she wondered if they might be in for a spot of off-roading. Maybe there was something wrong with her that she found that exciting when, by rights, she should have been a bit more put off by this man who'd swept her off to a foreign country without blinking an eye.

Wasn't *he* lucky that she carried her passport as a matter of course when she got on a plane, on the off chance she might be seized with the urge—and blessed with the funds—to fly to the Maldives.

Lillie assured herself now that she was *well ready* to get stern with him if necessary, should any of this suddenly seem less glamorous and more, well, anything else—

But instead she found herself gazing out the window beside her, the lovely, bright afternoon sunshine making her want to sigh with the pleasure of it. It was so dark and cold in Scotland this time of year. This past weekend had been the annual Christmas lights switch-on parade in Aberdeen. Lillie loved the holiday season. She loved the parade with Santas on scooters and all the choirs singing and the lights coming on, bright as you like, to make at least a small dent in the thick fall darkness.

Yet the lights over Union Street had nothing on the Portuguese sun.

Tiago sat beside her in the back of the SUV, looking up now and again from the mobile where he was typing rapidly—just in case she'd forgotten for even a moment that he was a very important and busy man. Not the pool boy at all. And so, not to be outdone, she pulled out her own mobile and fired off a few texts of her own—mostly to her housemates, reminding them that there were garbage bins to take out and rent money to start getting together for the first of December, and it felt better than she'd ever thought it would to remind them that she would not be taking responsibility for such things moving forward.

Might be a good idea to elect one of your lot to take over these duties, or see to that cleaning rota chart I suggested last summer.

She attached a smiley face, because that was how they liked to communicate unpleasant things to her, like the fact they wanted her out by Hogmanay so the new, age-appropriate housemate could move in by the time the new year had been adequately celebrated on the second of January.

And then she felt better still when the responses started coming in, most seeming *deeply shocked* that they could hold meetings to make her move out and then expect her to carry on playing the part of house mum all the same.

When she stuck her phone back in the pocket of her coat, she found Tiago studying her from across the car's back seat that had, until that moment, seemed spacious indeed.

Now it felt…close. And much hotter than it should have been, with the cold air from the vents blowing on her suddenly too-warm face.

"You look pleased with yourself," he observed, as if he'd been studying her, a notion that did not make her feel any cooler.

"Have you lived with a great many housemates? In shared accommodation?" They were following a long, narrow drive between high walls. There were olive trees hanging overhead, moss and vines creeping this way and that, and the walls' ancient granite caught the sun. It looked magical. It looked as if they might drive straight on into Narnia, and if they did, Lillie would not have been at all surprised. "I'm guessing not."

"When I was at university I lived in a house with some friends," he said after a moment, as if he would have preferred not to share that. As if it was a deeply personal bit of information to tell her that he had once shared a home with anyone. Or maybe the personal part was that he'd once had friends and, presumably, still did. Like a regular man instead of a *world-famous billionaire* who had *private jets* and the like. "I much preferred that to living in halls."

"Then you know they can take a bit of managing." She smiled, because dispensing with a role she'd outgrown long since felt *so good* that she was forced to wonder why on earth she'd taken this long to do it. Maybe this unexpected trip to the closest thing she'd ever seen to Narnia was, at last, the proper start to the new life she'd promised herself five months back. Maybe this was her chance to step straight in instead of *waffling* about it and carrying on the same as ever. Because one way or another, everything was changing. What if this was her chance to *choose* a few of those changes? Lillie made her smile a bit wider. "I've resigned as manager, effective immediately. And while they were happy enough to rid themselves of the pregnant woman making things awkward in the house, by existing apparently, they really didn't think through the fact that now someone else will have to step in and see to the managing. Is it wrong that I'm enjoying it?"

It wasn't that she'd forgotten his eyes, because she hadn't forgotten a single thing about him. She doubted she could or ever would. The trouble with them was that they were not quite blue, not quite green. And that looking at them felt like falling from a great height, or possibly flying, and somehow bracing for it didn't make it any better.

But she would be lying if she tried to tell herself she didn't like that soaring sensation.

He gazed at her for a long moment, as if shocked she'd asked him to weigh in on her prosaic concerns. She wasn't sure why she had, but she didn't take it back. "I do not think it is ever wrong to allow others to marinate in the consequences of their actions," he told her, as if measuring each word. Then he inclined his head. "Nor to enjoy it when they do, if only privately."

"Thank you." Lillie smiled wider, that soaring

feeling getting even more intense when she did. "That's vindicating."

The steep walls gave way, opening up over views of tidy vineyards and whitewashed buildings with red-tiled roofs. At first she thought they'd come to some kind of village. Then she realized that no, all the buildings had the same crest on their walls. The crest she'd seen behind Tiago in the news program, and all over his offices. This must all be his.

She felt something inside her shift, hard, as she stared out at the sun and the vineyards and the trees in the distance. How far did it go, this land of his? Was it possible he truly owned…everything?

Lillie couldn't quite get her head around it.

They were back to the narrow lane with high walls again, rounding a tight curve that had her closing her eyes for fear they'd crash head-on into oncoming traffic—but when there was no screeching of brakes or the like, she opened up her eyes again.

The SUV shot out of the shadows into another dazzling bit of light, and that was when the house came into view.

Once again, she had no idea how she managed to keep her jaw from dropping.

Because it wasn't a proper *house* at all. It wasn't a tidy semidetached in a quiet village like the one she'd grown up in. It wasn't Catriona's flat on the top floor of a converted row of terraces. It wasn't even one of those tarted-up houses out in Bielside, where all the flash oil and gas men lived and various royal personages were said to have once visited.

The place went on and on, terraces and balconies, pools and gardens, all arranged around a magnificent multileveled home that commanded the hillside it stood upon and looked out at the surrounding area like a conquering hero. It was like a private palace, and Tiago wasn't even looking at it. He wasn't sat there, poised for her reaction—that was how commonplace it all was to him, she realized.

This was when it began to really hit home how wealthy the man really was.

"How did you find this place?" she asked, because it was that or succumb to the wild buzzing in her ears. And because it sounded like the right sort of thing to ask.

Appropriately neutral, she thought.

He looked at her, too much blue and green. "Portugal?"

Lillie could hear from that carefully blank undercurrent in his voice that it was a stupid question after all. But all she did was gaze back at him, as if daring him to say so.

And she thought she saw the hint of a smile move over his face, after a moment or two, when there'd been very little of that since she'd tracked him down. But it was only a flash, so quick she wasn't sure that it was real. It was far more likely that she *wanted* to see him smile and that she'd made it up because it made her feel better to think he might.

That he might be as captivated with her now as he'd been that night.

Don't be foolish, she lectured herself. *This is about the baby, not you.*

And if she was a decent person and had the faintest hope of being a good mother, she wouldn't need it to be about anything more than that, would she?

"My mother's family are Portuguese," he was saying, once again in that careful, deliberate way of his. As if words were a precious resource and he intended to cultivate each and every one of them. "This land has been in her family some generations. The Villelas, as perhaps you know, maintain our ancestral presence in Spain."

"Fascinating," Lillie said, wrinkling up her nose. "The Mertons have maintained our ancestral presence in Scotland as well, though the thatched huts of us peasants don't stand up to the test of time nearly as well as ye olde family pile."

And once again, he looked startled. As if she'd surprised him.

But not, she thought after a moment, in a *bad* way. Necessarily.

Because once again, she thought she saw the hint of a smile on that marvelously rock-hard jaw of his. And it was clear to her that she was becoming a little too enamored of that. By this notion that she could actually burrow down beneath his skin in some way. *Disrupt* him, even.

Hadn't that been what had happened that night? She wouldn't have put it into those words. She hadn't. But that was what he had said himself in that hotel room in Spain. Again and again. *What have you done to me? What sort of sorceress are you?*

She'd thought it no more than a bit of flowery language—or anyway, she'd told herself it was, in retrospect. While ordering herself to forget about him.

But now she had to wonder if this man really went about living out his life with no one to tease him a bit. She thought that was sad. Lillie was fully aware that she'd let her own life get a bit sad, these last few years. It was just that she hadn't felt that overarching need to change things the way all her friends had, one after the next. She hadn't felt pulled to anything the way they had.

That was what happened when a person was raised in the shadow of a great love story. It made all else pale in comparison. Lillie had been conditioned to seek out her passions—but she hadn't exactly tripped over loads of passions lying about in the course of her life, had she?

While they'd all lived in the house, everything had been a grand old laugh, and that had seemed quite grand enough, for a time. Even now, though the lot of them were rarely able to get together as a group any longer, any time she visited one or the other of them it was always the same. The old jokes, the endless laughter, the sheer delight in poking at each other. It was one of the things that made life worth living, as far she could tell, whether there were passions aplenty or not.

Yet unless she was mistaken, it was all new to Tiago.

Because apparently the personal palace and endless vineyards and *private jets* weren't quite the laugh they seemed from afar.

"You came with no luggage," he said as the car pulled up to a stop in front of the grand entry. Or perhaps it was the servants' back entrance. How was Lillie meant to know the difference on such a grand scale? "I've taken the liberty of instructing my staff to provide you with a wardrobe during your stay. I hope that is not too impertinent."

"How do you know what size I wear?" she asked without thinking.

His blue-green gaze changed, then. It went dark like a sudden storm and her breath stopped.

She knew she shouldn't have asked that. Because Lillie knew exactly how he knew her proportions. She knew that he had taken her measure, inch by glorious inch. That it was likely he was the only person alive who knew her body better than she did.

Of course, now she also knew that he remembered that night in at least as much detail as she did.

"When in doubt," he said quietly into the thunder that rumbled—waiting just out of reach—between them, "I told them to err on the side of accommodating the changes your body has gone through since last I saw you."

That was such an innocuous sort of thing to say, wasn't it? There was no reason at all that her throat should go dry. That she could feel her breasts press insistently against the fabric of her dress. There was no reason at all that it should all feel like a sensual assault, leaving her breathless and doing her level best to ignore the slickness and heat between her legs.

Worse, she felt certain he knew exactly what she was trying to ignore.

Down to the slightest, faintest sensation. He knew.

For a moment, she thought that the storm hovering *right there* would blow her away. That they would be caught up, once more. That all of that lightning and longing would crash over them and light them up the way it had in Spain—

But instead, his gaze shuttered. He looked away.

And in the next moment, the doors of the car were opening and she had no choice but to get out after him and try her best to hide her reaction.

Out there in all that bright, revealing sunshine.

"This is my family's long-term housekeeper, Leonor," Tiago announced with some formality there by the side of the SUV. He beckoned an older woman closer and Lillie realized with a start that she hadn't paid the slightest bit of attention to anything but him. She hadn't even noticed the staff who waited for them, arranged in lines before a set of great doors that were flung wide open, presumably to receive the master of the house.

She ordered herself to get her body back under control before she made a complete fool of herself, because surely all this sunshine meant that everyone staring at her could *see* her reaction to this man. Surely they could feel that same storm approaching, the same as she could, and could track it *on her*.

But it was hard to keep her mind on such horrors, because she was hot. The sun was glaring down, her body was still reacting to the way he'd looked at her inside the car, and it was all too much. She found herself shrugging out of her favorite big coat that doubled as a cozy blanket in a pinch, only stopping when she heard a murmur of reaction from the waiting staff.

Tiago looked at them, then looked at her and the obvious bump that was her belly, and was that… dismay she saw move through his gaze? Pride in all that distracting blue and green?

But she couldn't tell, for it, too, was gone too quickly.

"I leave you in Leonor's capable hands," Tiago said, when there were so many other things he could have said. So many other things she wished he would

have said. Then he did something with his head that
put Lillie in mind of a bow.

It was quick, and then he turned and marched
toward the grand doors, all of his staff trailing behind him after a few rapid commands in what she
assumed was Portuguese.

What she noticed most of all was that he didn't
look back.

"If you will come with me, madam," Leonor said,
though Lillie was not fooled by her overtly polite
tone. Not when she could see the glint of steel in the
old woman's eyes.

Lillie aimed a big smile her way, and tried her best
to look sheepish, or docile. Or whatever it was that
would be expected of her, since Tiago hadn't seen
fit to offer her any instructions.

The old woman's brows arched up, but she said
nothing. She only did a version of that head-only
bow herself, then led the way into the waiting house.

Unsurprisingly, it was a dazzling affair. Airy,
open rooms that let the sunlight in on every side.
White walls, exposed beams, tiles and mosaics
everywhere. There was even a wide, center courtyard that was its own lush garden.

"This is beautiful," Lillie breathed, staring at the
flower—*flowers!*—that were blooming right there
before her this close to December.

"Senhor Villela's grandmother loved nothing
more than her plants," the housekeeper told her, with

what sounded like pride. "In her later years, she became obsessed with orchids and grew them here in our mild climate. She could often be found here, chatting with the bees and the birds, and singing to her flowers. We like to think that sometimes, she can still be felt here. Or heard singing on the breeze."

"What a lovely notion," Lillie said quietly, drinking in the bright colors and so much green.

And she wasn't sure she understood the assessing way the other woman looked at her then, so she pretended not to see it.

Instead she followed Leonor through the rest of the sprawling house, crossing through the courtyard and then heading out into the wing that waited on the far side. Lillie didn't know where to look. At the stunning furnishings, clearly placed just so, that very clearly utilized interior design elements that she'd only ever read about in magazines. Every room had its own specific character, she thought, yet was clearly a part of the whole—and each one was inviting. There were windows everywhere and skylights, too. The walls were filled with art, and though she couldn't identify any of the paintings, it seemed clear that each and every one of them had been chosen as much for the mastery of the artist as a particular enjoyment of what had been painted.

"Your rooms will have everything you need, I'm sure," Leonor said with a certain serene confidence as they walked down yet another hallway. "You are welcome to enjoy the rest of the guest wing as well. It has its own small library and a media room, should the private one in your rooms prove insufficient. Down at that end—" she nodded off toward what looked like nothing but a great wash of light down the length of the hall "—there is a patio that leads to a small pool that you may use exclusively while you are here. There is also a well-equipped gym, if that is your preference. If you wish to ride, you need only ring the stables to let them know you're coming, so that they might be prepared for you. And, naturally, you are welcome to walk wherever you please on the property."

Lillie could hardly take all that in. So she simply nodded, as if she spent every day of her life being offered such luxuries so offhandedly and stopped when the older woman did, just outside the first room along the hall.

Leonor flung open the doors and strode inside, leaving Lillie to trail after her. She saw quickly that she hadn't misheard. The housekeeper had said *rooms*, plural. There was a vast yet comfortable lounge with enough seating to fit an army, then what looked like a bit of an office space, complete with a computer and some other corporate-looking appliances. Another sort of sitting room a bit farther along opened up into a whole walk-in closet *complex* comprising three separate rooms, a sprawling en suite bathroom with a separate area for a bath with a view, and then, at the very end, the bedroom.

Which was, not to put too fine a point on it, much bigger than the entire ground floor of her house in Aberdeen, complete with the shared lounge and kitchen.

The room had a fireplace on one end, its own sitting area, and the most over-the-top four-poster bed she'd ever seen.

"I hope this will suffice," Leonor intoned.

"Yes," Lillie said, somehow managing not to laugh out loud at the notion there might be anyone alive who would find this *insufficient*. She tried to look posh. "It should do."

And when the other woman left her there, saying something about leaving her to settle in, Lillie finally broke. She burst into a helpless sort of laughter. She laughed and laughed, clinging to the nearest post at the foot of the bed until she felt weak and tears were streaming down her face. Then, gingerly—a bit as if she expected armed guards to burst in and carry her away—she crawled up onto the bed, and began laughing all over again. Because the mattress was soft as a feather and she had never felt anything like it. It was tempting to believe they slept on *actual clouds* here.

It was *so* soft, and so clearly elegant, and smelled ever so faintly like lavender and far fancier herbs besides, that Lillie doubted very much that she'd be able to actually drift off to sleep surrounded by such class—

And so was surprised to find herself blinking awake some time later.

The position of the light and shadows in the room suggested she'd slept a good while. She pushed herself up onto her elbows, frowning and cranky, the way she always was after a nap. Her cheeks felt flushed too hot and she had to shove her damp curls back out of her face, quite certain that she'd slept hard the way she always did. As if felled by a huntsman's ax.

She heard faint sounds from somewhere outside this room and everything inside her leaped a bit, with his name inside her like its own dancing bit of flame.

Tiago.

And as she swung her feet off the side of the bed, not at all surprised to find she'd slept with her boots still on, the rest of the day came flooding back to her. Tiago himself. Seeing him again in his office in London. That ridiculously fancy plane. This house that was its own city, it was so large.

The way everything had sparked between them again in the car—though Lillie wasn't sure how she felt about that. She was happy that she hadn't made the whole thing up, the way she'd tried so hard to convince herself she had all these months. Or if it actually only hurt more, because now she knew it was real.

But she also *knew that it was real*. Without question. And she also knew where he was.

Though as she got to her feet, rubbing her palms over her face and heading toward that soft noise she'd heard, she had to question that, too. *Did* she know where he was? This was a very large house in what appeared to be its very own countryside, for one thing. Not to mention, he also had his own plane. He could be anywhere.

But she found she couldn't follow that up the way she wanted to, because when she emerged into that sitting room she'd seen when she first walked into her rooms, Leonor was standing there overseeing the staff as they laid out a meal for her.

And it turned out that she was ravenously hungry.

"I hope you enjoy what the cook has prepared," the housekeeper said, standing to the side of the table near the window, looking…assessing, yet again. "Some local delicacies have been prepared alongside what we consider more typical fare for you."

"A bit of haggis, then?" Lillie asked with a laugh and then regretted it, because the other woman only gazed back at her.

"Please make yourself at home in this wing," she said in that excessively calm manner of hers. "Relax however you see fit, refresh yourself after your journey, and I will come to you in the morning."

It was not until after Lillie had polished off enough food to feed a football team or two that she realized that Leonor had obliquely suggested that she stay put. That she confine herself to this wing, in fact.

But Lillie…had not agreed to that, had she?

She went and availed herself of that glorious bathroom, rinsing off the travel and the nap and her feast. Unable to help herself, she went and peeked into the wardrobe, and found that Tiago—or his staff, it was almost certainly his *staff*—really had thought of everything. And more, that every single item of clothing that hung in all three rooms of that walk-in closet *complex* was exactly the sort of thing that Lillie would have chosen for herself.

If, that was, she had ever had unlimited funds at her disposal.

And though she had considered herself practical and frugal the whole of her life, it turned out that all it took was two good meals and a well-stocked closet and Lillie was nothing but a silly little madam after all, more than happy to play dress-up.

But when she finished with that, and was wearing the kind of outfit that once would have made her laugh because it was so out of her usual reach, she set off out of her rooms. Plural. She looked down the hall toward the bit that led to all the parts of the great, big house that weren't a part of the guest wing, and decided that what she really wanted to do on her first night in Portugal was a spot of exploring.

"It has nothing to do with Tiago," she told herself

virtuously. And loud enough to bounce back at her from the quiet, likely reproachful walls. "I just want to get a sense of the place."

And she kept right on lying to herself as she set off, *absolutely not* looking for him at all.

CHAPTER FOUR

TIAGO DID NOT come to the house in Portugal as much as he had as a child, when he had spent a great many school holidays here with his grandmother. And then, after both she and his mother were gone, his father had switched off and on between this estate and the Villela land in Spain so he would be familiar with them both.

Yet these days he spent more time in London than anywhere else, so he could be closer to the office.

But he still knew every single sound that the old house could possibly make. The rattle of the breeze against the windows. The rustle of the trees outside. The way the wind moved in the courtyard that a fanciful person might imagine was an old woman, still murmuring to the flowers she'd loved to tend.

Not that Tiago allowed himself any such flights of fancy.

On this late November night, Tiago had repaired to the office that had once belonged to his grandfather and still smelled faintly of cigars and port. He sat in the old leather armchair where the old man had napped away his later years and found himself brooding in the general direction of his grandfather's bookcase. It was packed tight with well-worn volumes of books that Tiago had been fascinated with when he was young. He'd thought the world of his grandfather. And he'd imagined that all he needed to do was read this particular selection of books and he would somehow find himself the same sort of man.

It was as close as he allowed himself to get to the memories of his grandparents he'd buried long ago, then packed down tight beneath the cool practicality that he'd been expected to embody. The composure that they had prized far above any leftover sentimentality that, these days, lived on only in the flowers out there in the courtyard.

Flowers he told himself he barely noticed some years.

But he had read all the books in this study, years ago now, and still the man *he* was had ignored every single lesson he'd ever been taught.

In so doing, he had failed to adequately protect both Lillie—and he still couldn't get enough of thinking that name, her *actual name* when she had been nameless in his head for far too long—and his own family legacy. The very thing he had sworn to protect, always.

Now she was pregnant with his child, his heir.

The future of his family was hanging in the balance. There were things he needed to do, and soon, in the wake of the knowledge she'd dropped on him today. There was no time for *brooding*.

But all he could think about was the night they'd shared in Spain. About the things that they could do stretched out across a bed, with nothing but their bodies moving together in the dark.

The things their bodies called out in each other, God help him.

He knew better than this. Those flowers remained not as a love letter to a grandmother long gone, but to remind him of what it had been like to give himself over to his jangling, discordant grief. He had sobbed, out in that courtyard in the rain, and his parents had left him there.

They had decamped to Spain for the rest of that season, leaving him to sort himself out—or, Leonor had told him with her usual serene demeanor despite the unusual gleam in her gaze, they would wash their hands of him.

And he had been just a boy. He had barely been able to process the loss of his favorite person, how could he lose his parents, too?

He had taught himself how to…put those things away.

To hide them as if they did not, could not, exist.

Until sometimes he believed they never had.

And thus tonight all he could do—all he would

allow himself to do—was stay where he was, frowning across the room at a bookcase that had been carefully filled by a far better man, listening to the sounds of the old house as the hour grew late around him.

He could hear the wind outside, coming in from the sea. There were the usual sounds of the old house settling into another night, the groundskeeper doing his rounds in his rattly old jeep, the staff opening and closing doors in the distance.

And yet when he heard footfalls in the hall outside the study, he told himself he was imagining it. At first.

Or he wanted to be imagining it, because no staff member moved like that. He knew that without question. They all moved swiftly and almost entirely silently. Not those meandering, hesitating steps down the length of the hall that led to this office, where everyone here knew he did not like to be disturbed.

Everyone except his guest, that was.

His guest. His Lillie.

Tiago still could not understand how this was happening. Not the mechanics. He remembered those all too well, and happily.

But he had never felt such things before. Even before today, she had consumed his thoughts and he had *felt things*. It was an outrage.

He had told himself for months now that was all a function of the fact that he could not have her. That if she'd been there in front of him, he would have been as disinterested as he normally was after enjoying a woman. He would have politely disengaged and never thought of her again.

At the moment, Tiago could barely imagine maintaining a polite veneer in front of Lillie, much less *disengaging* with her. Hell, he'd brought her here, to the one place on earth he considered some kind of sanctuary, where no one who was family or someone hired by the family had set foot in ages.

Perhaps he had been lying to himself all this time.

He scowled at the books, seeing not a single one of the old, cracked, much-loved spines. He was thinking instead of Lillie moving over him in that bed in Spain, rocking her hips against his in that maddeningly lush rhythm that had undone him. He was remembering her back arched in a perfect bow, her head thrown back, and all those glorious curls moving with her.

And when he shifted his gaze to the door once more, she was there.

Quite as if he had summoned her—though Tiago already knew too well that despite his best efforts, that never worked.

It never had before.

"Oh." She looked as startled as she sounded, but he drank her in as if she was a dose of clear, sweet water and he had been wandering for five some

months in a barren desert. He felt as if that was no more than the simple truth. "Tiago."

Her hair was haphazardly pinned up on the top of her head, as if she'd tossed it up and forgotten all about it. And he was a sophisticated man. He attended formal black-tie events as a matter of course, ate at the finest restaurants, and normally dated women who were renowned for their beauty and elegance above all else.

Yet this was the one who seemed to have taken up all the space inside his chest. With that wild hair and her siren's eyes, too much like the sea.

She had changed into soft-looking lounging pants, obviously made of the finest cashmere with what looked like a touch of merino wool for structure, and the sort of T-shirt that looked defiantly simple yet was cut by artisans to make her curves into a song.

And there was no denying what he had already noticed—that he had found her astounding before, in Spain, but this new ripeness of hers might very well be his undoing.

When he was not a man who could be *undone*. Everything in his life forbade it.

"I'm sorry if I'm intruding," she was saying, though she did not appear particularly apologetic, to his eye. "I was exploring."

"I feel certain I made it clear that you were to be kept to your wing of the house," he said, softly enough. And perhaps she could hear the menace in his tone. Or perhaps she had no experience with such things and couldn't identify it when she heard it.

Whatever it was, she seemed unfazed. He was unused to...*not* eliciting reactions wherever he happened to find himself.

"What a lovely house," she said instead. "I can't wait to walk around tomorrow and pay more attention to the view. It must be epic."

"Lillie." And he meant to cut her off. To cut her down to size while he was at it. But instead, just as it had in Spain, his gaze...got caught. On her.

And he couldn't seem to do a thing about it.

Because nothing in his life before or since had prepared him for the sight of her, like a sledgehammer, as he'd walked through that crowded pool area, and had seen her there.

He still wasn't prepared.

Tiago found himself on his feet and moving toward her. When he knew that what he wanted to do was stay put. Keep his distance. That was what he *needed* to do. At the very least, it would be wise to avoid these interactions with her until ground rules were set out, contracts signed, and the way forward carefully plotted out and wholly understood by both parties.

What he could not understand was why this woman was the one thing on the whole of the earth that made him reckless.

And maybe she was reckless too, because surely

a wise creature would take one look at him in this current, dangerous mood he was in, turn, and run.

But Lillie, *his Lillie*, stayed where she was. She leaned against one side of the open doorway, doing nothing at all but gazing back at him as he prowled toward her.

Tiago wished that she would say something. Point out that he should not think that he could so easily hide her away here. Fight with him. Yell at him. Hold him to account for getting her pregnant in the first place, and leaving her no possible way of finding him again.

Why didn't she do any of these things?

But as he came to a stop before her, he knew.

He had never asked for this ability to read her, this strange woman he still barely knew. But he could.

Just as he had once before.

And so he knew that it wasn't that she didn't feel all of those things. She did. It was that she felt other things far more.

Damn her.

But even as he thought that, he was moving again. Closer. Much closer.

This time to do the very thing he shouldn't, but he seemed to have no ability whatever to stop.

His hand slipped under the hem of her T-shirt, then smoothed its way over that high, round ball of her belly, finding her skin satiny and hot. And then, as he kept his hands there, he felt her shiver, too.

"You are carrying my child," he said, his voice a mere scrape across the space between them.

Her eyes were wide, her lips slightly parted, and for once she did not laugh. "I am."

"I want to be furious," he told her, or perhaps he was confessing to the bump he held between his palms. "I want to rage, throw things, break whatever I get my hands upon."

"I know," she whispered. "I wanted to be angry. Ashamed. But instead… Tiago…"

Something inside him felt as if it was cracking. Falling apart, crumbling—

And he knew he didn't want her to finish that sentence.

He didn't know why he'd started it.

So instead of continuing down this dangerous road that could not lead them anywhere good, he dropped his head and fit his mouth to hers.

And that, too, would have knocked him back if he hadn't been holding on to her.

Because it turned out that he hadn't been telling himself fairy stories about what it was like to kiss this woman.

She tasted like every dream he'd had about her since, and better yet.

Because she kissed him as if she'd been waiting her whole life to do nothing else. She kissed him as if they'd been crafted for this, hewn from flesh and blood precisely to drive each other mad.

And so, for those sweet, breathless moments, that was what they did.

She licked into his mouth. He angled his jaw, one hand going to slide along the side of her face, to hold her where he wanted her. To keep it hot like this. Wild and perfect and wholly theirs.

It was as if no time had passed. As if this was that morning after that they had been denied in Spain.

As if nothing had ever or could ever keep them apart.

He made a low noise in the back of his throat and moved closer, so that his body was pressed to hers again. *At last.* And Tiago exulted in the parts of her that would change even more, the parts that were already pressed up flush against him.

The changes that *he* had made in her.

Both of his hands moved to cup her face, his fingers spearing into her hair, exulting in those curls that clung to him as every strand wanted him as badly as he wanted her. And as he took the kiss deeper, more carnal, he found nothing but magic in her taste.

Just as he remembered it. As he remembered *her*.

She kissed him back the same way, her hands sneaking up to lace around his neck, and this was how it had started last summer. This was how it had ended up here, with the proud jut of the baby they'd made between them even now.

One kiss, and then everything had bloomed into

brilliant golds and fiery reds, and he hadn't had another coherent thought since.

Not where she was concerned.

And yet that, ironically enough, was what got through to him.

He tore his lips from hers, though everything in him resisted such violence. And for a moment, because he could not make himself step back the way he should have, he rested his head against hers.

Sharing her air. Exulting in the way she breathed. Taking pleasure in the way her breasts shuddered against his chest.

It took him far longer than it should have to disengage entirely and move back.

"That cannot happen again," he told her. Severely.

"It seems likely to happen again and again and again," she replied after a moment, her voice husky. Roughened in a way that made him want nothing more than to lay her out before the fire crackling in his grate, follow her down to the ground, and see if it was even possible to indulge in her enough that this hunger might somehow be sated. "Otherwise, I don't see why you transported me all the way to this lovely, remote estate where no one could possibly hope to find me."

"I am afraid you have the wrong idea."

And he heard the way he said that. So stiff, so unyielding, that he might as well have been made of stone. He sounded like every lecture his father had ever given him. All that talk of duty, legacy. Responsibility. Until tonight, he had always thought those things were stamped deep on his bones. That he would not need to think of them, for he simply *was* them.

In every possible respect, it seemed, except where she was concerned.

Tiago expected her to react badly to what he said. To look hurt, at the very least. He braced himself for it, not sure that he would be able to handle it the way he needed to, but already lecturing himself on why it was necessary that things be done in the way he had decided earlier.

But Lillie laughed. "You think I've got the wrong idea, do you?" Her laughter was not helpful. It was like a bright song, filling the room and pouring through him, like the melody a wish might make as it was granted. "Do you reckon? I'm nearly five months pregnant. What *wrong idea* do you imagine I might have?"

"I intended to have a discussion with you tomorrow," he said, even more stiffly than before, as if he was an awkward man. As if there had ever been a situation that he could not master.

This was the first. He disliked it, intensely.

Her brows arched as she studied him. And though she laughed again, it seemed less an expression of pure amusement—not with that new edge to it. She crossed her arms, her siren eyes looking narrower than before.

He didn't like that either.

"I've ruined everything by not staying locked up in my room like a naughty child, clearly," she said, and then she even rolled her eyes. As if that was something people could just...*do* at him. "You really don't seem to like it much when things don't go according to your plan, do you? I expect that's all the money. It makes a person imagine that everything they think and do is more important. And that if others don't fall in line, that it's necessary to maneuver them into whatever it is you think they should do. No one likes to be maneuvered, Tiago. Maybe you don't know that, having grown up like this. I accept that it's possible no one has told you. Likely because they work for you and are too scared to tell you much of anything, if you want my opinion."

"I do not," he grated out. "And as it happens, Lillie, you are the only thing that has ever failed to go according to plan."

She didn't ask him if he meant tonight, or five months ago. But then, he knew she didn't need to. Because he knew that she possessed the same confounding skill that he did, but in reverse. He knew this woman was perhaps the only person alive who could read him with a glance.

He didn't care for that, either. But he comforted himself that at least he wasn't meeting her in a delicate contract negotiation where his ability to bluff his way into a better position would be at risk.

"I hope you don't think I'm going to apologize for that," she said, after spending too long looking for God only knew what on his face. "Besides, this is all you playing catch-up. I can assure you, falling pregnant after one night on a Spanish vacation was not in my plans, either. And until yesterday, I assumed that was a responsibility I'd be taking on all alone."

"That obviously won't be necessary." He could *taste* her, was the thing. That made it feel like nothing short of an indignity that he could not go to her, strip her naked, and taste her everywhere else, too. But he didn't do it. Somehow. He moved, though his body felt as if it was fighting him every step of the way, and located himself behind the desk over against one wall. So he could at least attempt to feel more in control. "I'm a man of limitless resources. There is no need for you to struggle ever again, and indeed, I intend to see to it that you do not."

But she did not look even remotely relieved. Or grateful. She scowled at him. "I didn't seek you out for a payday."

Tiago raised a brow. "Did you not? Then you would be the first."

"I sought you out," she said, very primly, "because it was *the right thing to do.*"

"And the fact that I am a wealthy man by any

standard played no part in your decision to turn up in my office, I am certain."

She stared at him for a moment, and he realized that she wasn't coming back at him with a knee-jerk response. It looked as if she was considering what he'd said. "No, you're right. I thought you were the pool boy, after all. It was a pleasant surprise to find that if you chose to take responsibility, this baby would be well looked after."

And that was what he wanted her to say, surely. It was what he'd expected her to say from the start. But now that she'd said it, he found it rang false. It sat in him wrong, and he had long considered himself a finely tuned instrument when it came to other people's veracity. It was part of what made him such an excellent businessman, capable of keeping his fingers in a great many pies at once, secure in the knowledge that it was a very difficult thing indeed for anyone to fool him.

He could not say that what he felt at the moment was *secure*.

"There is obviously a great deal of chemistry between us," he said baldly, because he was always good at that, too. Never one for messing about with thinly veiled this and implications of that, not when he could aim straight at it instead. He saw her eyes widen and could not have said if the sensation that seemed to punch through him was delight that he had gained ground, or a strange regret. "But that is not something I choose to indulge in when it comes to matters of business."

"Matters of business?" she echoed, sounding as if she *wanted* to laugh but couldn't quite get there. "Are you referring to your child as part of your… business?"

"The child will not simply be a baby, Lillie." He sounded forbidding, he knew, but he leaned into it. Because she needed to hear this. She needed to fully take the reality of the situation on board. "This child will be the heir to two great dynasties. Both come with their own august legacies and considerable mythologies, which would be burden enough. But both also come with significant fortunes attached, and that, like it or not, is business. For if it is not, it will soon be a moot point. It will all disappear. The work of generations, that easily."

There was something in her gaze then, making all that bright blue turn dark. "What exactly are you trying to say to me?"

Tiago sighed, as if she was being dense. And he hated himself for that, too, when she stiffened. "This cannot be an affair, Lillie. No matter what happened between us in Spain. Do you not understand? I will have to marry you."

Her eyes went wide. Her face paled, and not, his ego could not help but note, in the transformative joy a man in his position might have expected to see after a proposal. "Marry me? Marry *you*? Are you mad? On the strength of one night?"

"On the strength of your pregnancy. Because the Villela heir must be legitimate." He looked at her as if he had never seen her before and would never see her again, or maybe it was simply that he did not wish to say the thing he knew he must. But that was life, was it not? Forever forcing himself to do what was necessary, what was right. Never what he wanted. So he took a deep breath. "We will marry. Quickly. And once that happens, I will never touch you again."

He didn't know what he expected her to do. Cry, perhaps. Look torn apart by such declaration.

Make it clear that she thought that was as much of an injustice as he did.

But instead she straightened against the doorjamb. Then she glared at him as if she was the one in charge here. As if she had the power.

"Good," she said, her eyes flashing. "Let's hurry up and marry, then."

CHAPTER FIVE

THE WEDDING TOOK place three days later.

And if Lillie was discomfited by the speed of it, and how clearly it had all been planned before they'd come to Portugal in the first place, that seemed to be the least of her worries. Primary among her actual concerns was…what had become of her.

In Scotland she'd been…diffident. Forgiving. She'd let all those idiots in her house condescend to her for ages. She'd let them get away with all that passive aggressiveness while she'd spent the last few years of her life adrift, because all of her actual friends had gone ahead and got lives while she hadn't had the slightest idea what to do with hers.

She had been asleep for years, perhaps, but she was wide awake now.

And she had to stay awake, because while *she* might have been worryingly happy to remain drifting to and fro in the tiny little tides of her little life, that was not the sort of life she wished to model for a child.

Once she started thinking like that, the stakes seemed even higher.

What sort of mother did her baby deserve?

Not the sort who let a scrum of housemates treat her ill, that was certain. And not the sort to bow down to the man who'd fathered her baby, either. She might have been spirited away to Tiago Villela's Portuguese retreat. She was pregnant with his child and set to marry him, fair enough.

That hadn't exactly been the proposal of her dreams, but *she* wasn't backing down, because being Tiago's—legally—was no more than *her* baby deserved, and Lillie had discovered to her delight that there were some things, it turned out, she was perfectly happy to fight about.

The life her child could and would have topped that list.

Leonor, who was clearly more family than housekeeper, assured her that everything was well in hand. All Lillie had been asked to do over the past few days was rest, eat, and entertain herself. All of which she had done, to excess.

A lot like she was trying to prove something to Tiago. How comfortable she was. How at her ease with his dictates.

Only when she was all alone, late at night, did she admit that the fact it was so easy for him to ignore the passion that still scorched her, just thinking of it, hurt her more than it should.

It was only there in her bed of clouds, covers over her head, could she let herself shake with all the pent-up *nerves* she dared not show to a man she'd thought was made of molten heat who, apparently, could *decide* to make himself an ice sculpture at will.

But when she woke up each morning, she allowed none of her bewilderment to show.

He didn't want to touch her? *Marvelous.* She could entertain herself without him forever. She found out quickly that most of the books in the house were languages she didn't speak. Portuguese, of course, but also Spanish, French, and what she thought was German. It was only in the guest wing that the books were in English. But because she had a stubborn streak, she liked to take books she could actually read and settle down to read them…in other parts of the house.

Because if no one was going to admit that Tiago wanted her to remain confined to quarters so he need not gaze upon her unless he expressly wished it, she was going to pretend she had no idea that she was supposed to stay put.

She swam in the pool that Leonor had pointed out to her that first night. Even though it was the waning days of November, the pool was warm, the sun was bright, and it was all much more delightful than it should have been.

Ice sculptures be damned.

They brought her a decadent high tea each day at four on the dot. Besides that, there were all the meals she could possibly want, the food so good it would have made her eyes roll back in her head in sheer delight…

But she was too busy pretending not to be affected by any of it. And all that pretending was a lot of work. It made her hungry.

It made her shake in her bed, night after night, when no one could see her.

Today, however, was her wedding day and she was finding it difficult to keep up the same stubborn front.

She felt fluttery and odd, she acknowledged, as she sat in the sitting room in her guest quarters to take her breakfast that morning. More fluttery by the moment.

"Maybe it's jitters," she told herself as she sipped at her tea.

Jitters were normal. They had to be, or there wouldn't be a name for them, would there? Though she'd never felt anything quite like them before. And she needed to talk herself out of them, or slap herself into shape, because she had no intention of appearing anything but calm and in control today.

Lillie was just starting the process with a sound internal lecture, when the door swung open and Tiago walked in.

"I'm sure I've heard that it's bad luck to see a bride before the wedding ceremony," she said, hoping it sounded as unwelcoming and self-contained as she wanted it to.

But even if it did, it was a wasted effort, because all Tiago did was help himself to one of the seats in the room. He settled into the comfortable couch across from her that he made seem entirely too small, and then fixed her with that mesmerizing gaze of his.

"There are a few things we must go over," he told her, as coldly as if they had never kissed. Much less spent a night naked and sweating, with him so deep inside of her she could still feel him now.

The flutters in her belly increased.

"Wonderful," she said, spearing a piece of sliced ham with more force than was perhaps warranted. Or perhaps not, she thought when she saw that he'd brought a whole sheaf of papers with him. "It's the romance for me."

He ignored that, but in a manner that suggested she was *gauche* for even mentioning *romance*. "In the coming months, we will pay far more attention to the intricacies of your role, but this is what I must impress upon you now. The Villelas do not and will not divorce. But that does not mean that there will be the sort of scandals that inevitably spill out into the pages of tawdry newspapers. You and I must never become fodder for tabloids, Lillie."

"No worries," she said blandly. "I've managed to avoid appearing in all the tabloids so far."

She got another cold look from Tiago, that was all. "My expectation is that this will function like any other business arrangement. We will both state our needs. We will negotiate until we reach an agreement. And we will abide by the conclusions we reach together. Do you understand?"

"You seem to be under the impression that I work for you," Lillie said, pleasantly enough. Conversationally, even. "I'm the woman you knocked up, Tiago. I don't actually owe you anything. The only reason I haven't run screaming from this house is because of the baby. The only thing that interests me is what might be good for this child. If that means the front page of every tabloid in the universe, I'll sign right up. Do *you* understand?"

And for a dizzying moment, she saw the Tiago she knew. The man with all that passion and wonder in his gaze, even if, this morning, it was less wonder and more indignation. Whatever it was, it wasn't *cold*.

She knew, then, that there was something in her that would do anything to bring them back here. Anything at all. No matter what it took.

Though in the next moment, she dismissed that. It was childish. It didn't matter what was going on *in his eyes*, for God's sake. What mattered was what she'd just told him mattered.

The baby, beginning and end.

"A Villela marriage is a business arrangement," he told her. Very much as if she hadn't said a word. "They are run to work in the mutual best interests of both parties, as agreed from the start."

"How charming."

"Things are different when there's so much money involved, Lillie." His tone was repressive then, but Lillie did not wish to be repressed. "I do not expect you to understand that, of course, but if your true interest is in the child, then it must be clear to you that making certain he or she is capable of assuming my position one day with as little scandal as possible can only be a good thing."

"I'm not signing anything," she told him.

She didn't know she was going to say that, but when she did, it felt a lot like shaking up a bottle of bubbly, popping the cork, and letting it spray all around. A mad sort of joy, in other words. So when he frowned at her, she lifted her chin and shrugged nonchalantly, as if this had been her plan all along.

"I must insist," Tiago said.

"It's not in my best interest," she replied, with a wave of her hand. The one holding the fork, so it looked like nothing so much as a scepter. "Whatever those papers are, they're not for me, are they? They're for you. So I'll have to decline. If you feel that we need to get married to protect this baby, that's fine. I'll do it. And not because I agree with the way you framed the whole thing. But because, obviously, having this baby born as your legitimate heir can only be good. For the baby."

"And, of course, for you."

"Are there benefits to being the wife of one of the richest men in the world?" she asked facetiously. "I guess we'll see. But if you were so worried about me getting my hands on all your wealth and consequence, you shouldn't have offered in the first place."

He sighed. "I think there's been a misunderstanding."

"The only misunderstanding is how you managed to act as if you were fully human while we were in Spain," she retorted, with enough heat that she surprised herself. "And now it turns out that you're nothing of the kind. You're not a man, you're…a *corporation*."

That gaze of his went glacial. "I beg your pardon?"

And for some reason that she couldn't have put into words, Lillie found that she was suddenly enjoying herself. "I mean, think about it from my perspective. I have a blisteringly hot night with a mysterious man on a Spanish holiday. And then, months later, accidentally see his face on the nightly news. As I happen to be pregnant with his child, I make an appointment to see him. Partly it was to see that he knew about the baby, as is only right. But the other part, naturally, was to see if that night was real. If

I'd made it all up in my head. And behold. It appears I did."

"Lillie."

And for a moment, she felt exhilarated. As if she'd somehow managed to goad him into…some kind of explosion that would bring back the Tiago she liked.

And, possibly, lead to more kissing.

Because she'd thought of little else since that night in his study.

But instead, he leaned forward, resting his elbows on his knees and letting his hands dangle. It made him look entirely too much like the man she'd just accused him of not being. "I can see that I've gone about this the wrong way."

And he sounded so reasonable, so relatable. It took her a moment to remember that this was literally his job. Making people believe him so that he could make even more money.

If the searches she'd done on him since she'd arrived here were true, he had a gift. He was that good at it.

You need to steel yourself against this man, lass, she told herself grimly.

But he was looking at her square. And there was nothing cold or arrogant on his face, which she told herself was yet another tell. He was putting on an act, surely. He had to be.

"The truth is that I'm just as concerned about the baby as you are," he told her and more, sounded as if he meant it. *Part of the act*, she assured herself. "I want to make sure that our child has all the protection that I can offer him, or her, and as quickly as possible. I think you're taking all this talk of marital business the wrong way. It isn't as if we won't have a good working relationship within the marriage, it's just that when it comes to what I have to offer you and the child, I think it's better to focus on the big-ticket items first. And also the realities."

Listening to him talk like this was dangerous. She found herself wanting to nod along and talk more about this *good working relationship.* To stand up from a little table and go to him, so she could sit beside him on the couch and perhaps put her hand on his, to make sure he knew that she was listening. Carefully. With her whole body—

You need to sort yourself right out, she told herself sternly.

"And I don't mean that these realities are a bad thing," he continued in the same seemingly earnest tone. "You and I barely know each other. We were together for one night, and I think we can both agree that it was…out of the ordinary. It can only make sense to hammer out an agreement that protects us both. Don't you think?"

"I do," Lillie shot back at him, with enough ferocity that he blinked. But she didn't walk it back. He was doing a job, but *she* was fighting for something. For her baby, for herself. She was *taking charge of her life*, for once. "But you can't imagine it makes sense that all that hammering out is being done by your attorneys. Who's looking out for me? And don't say you." She made herself smile, despite the quick clatter of her pulse. Especially when he looked as if it troubled him that she would make such an accusation, when she hadn't even properly made it yet. "Even if you're the kindest, most self-sacrificing person in the world, it would make sense for me to verify that, wouldn't it? Not simply trust you blindly."

"Lillie," he said in that quiet, intense way of his. "I want you to marry me. Today."

And she knew, at once, that she was lying to herself. That for all her noble intentions of doing this, that, or the other *thing for the child*, what it all came down to was this.

The way her heart beat even faster when he said that. The way she reacted when she was near him. Her nipples stood at attention. Between her legs, she could feel his voice the way she'd once felt his tongue, licking into her.

The truth of the matter, whether she wished to admit it to herself or not, was that she was a right fool where this man was concerned.

Or she would have sent him a letter, as he'd said. An email. She could have called. She wouldn't have turned up in his office, kitted out in a nice dress and her best boots, would she?

"I want you to marry me," he told her again, his

blue-green gaze even more intense. "But I also need it. Tell me what I have to do to get you to sign this agreement. Name your terms and I will make them happen. That's how important it is to me that we secure our child's future. Today."

She thought about the phone call she'd had with her parents the day after he'd announced they would marry and how overjoyed they'd been that she was attempting to work things out with the father of the baby.

Is he a good sort? her father had asked, obviously doubtful from the get-go, given the last they'd talked.

He's not a bad *sort, if that's what you mean*, she'd replied. *Though it's early days.*

Women have been handling the fathers of their unexpected babies since the dawn of time, her mother had said with a laugh. *All it takes is as much honey as vinegar, darling. And a little bit of backbone while you're at it.*

Lillie did not ask her mother how she knew that, since she and Lillie's dad had met in primary school and had been inseparable ever since. *It was always a matter of when, not if, we'd have you, love*, they'd told her.

But the important thing about her parents' marriage was that it was a very, very good one. It was clear to anyone who encountered them that they doted on each other. That they were fond of each other, day in and day out. They had always laughed more than her friends' parents did. They held hands, still. Her father brought her mother cups of tea every morning. She cooked him his favorite meals every night. They sat at the kitchen table and talked well into the night at least once a week. They locked their bedroom door when they were in it, still.

They would have been embarrassed to call what they had *a great love*, but Lillie knew that was what it was. She had felt it. She was *part* of it.

Maybe it didn't matter how a thing started. Maybe what mattered was how it went along.

Or maybe, Lillie countered herself in her head, *you're just delusional enough to imagine that no matter what this man thinks he feels, you can change it.*

But when she looked at him across from her, she wondered about that, too.

Maybe she wasn't delusional at all. Because Tiago could talk all he liked about business this and no touching that, and all the rest of it besides, but he hadn't kissed her as if he cared about any of those things.

And at the end of the day, what was her alternative? Her cousin's spare room when her child could be the heir to all of this? For the sake of her pride?

How could she think she could call herself a good mother if she did something like that?

So she tilted her head a little bit to one side, though she couldn't quite manage to be as flippant as she wanted.

"Well," she said, and had to swallow, hard. "Since you asked so nicely, I will. I'll marry you."

And because he smiled at her, she even signed his papers, too.

Because what she wanted was a father for her child. She wasn't a gold digger. She hadn't had the slightest idea there was any gold to dig. That being the case, she didn't see any reason why she *shouldn't* sign. How silly would it be to turn around and make some claim to this land, this house, this grand legacy for herself?

For her child, now—that was a different story.

So she signed the papers. And she stood in his study with the celebrant from the local registrar, the notary, the unreadable Leonor, and several other officials who might actually have been his attorneys, and she married him.

"That was not exactly the culmination of love's young dream," she said not long after, when the official-looking men had all been ushered out by the housekeeper and only she and Tiago remained. "But I suppose it got the job done."

Because she was trying to sound supportive.

He glanced over at her, this man who was her *husband*—a word that felt silly to even *think*—and Lillie told herself it was just as well that they'd done it this way. There was no big white dress. No crowds of family or friends. No flowers, no attempt at emotional vows, no deeply embarrassing yet always entertaining wedding disco.

He was wearing what she supposed was a more casual version of his usual clothing. The usual dark suit, but the collar of his crisp white shirt was open. Wide enough that she could see not only the strong column of his throat, but the hint of the dark hair she knew was sprinkled over his chest—seeming to exist purely to emphasize the marvelous shape of him. Those hard planes of muscle, the intriguing ridges of his abdomen.

Though it was better not to think of such things right now, she warned herself. She looked down at her own outfit instead, a simple dress from her suddenly expansive wardrobe. Deceptively simple, that was. She knew perfectly well that it made her look somehow delicate and elegant at once, when she felt more awkward and misshapen by the day.

And instead of being bridal in any regard, it was a serviceable navy.

Yet they were married all the same.

Tiago kept looking at her intently far too long. And then he beckoned for her to follow him as he opened up the floor-to-ceiling windows that were everywhere in this house, all of them doubling as doors that let out to the various tiers of terraces and balconies and patios aplenty. In this case, the red-tiled patio was set beneath an arbor, trailing vines that might not have been flowering in the first flush of spring, but were pretty all the same.

Though all Lillie could think of was how pretty they would look if she accentuated them with some Christmas lights. Out here, in all this winter sunshine, it seemed entirely too easy to forget what day it was. What month. She supposed that if she didn't have a baby growing inside her to mark the time it would be the easiest thing in the world to simply drift off into a daydream of some eternal Portuguese summer and lose touch with herself entirely. It was already difficult to imagine that there was any scenario that would lead her to return to all that cold hard rock in Aberdeen.

Tiago ushered her to a seat at the table that had been set up there, waiting for them.

"How lovely to have a bit of a meal after a wedding," Lillie said brightly. "Almost makes it seem real, doesn't it?"

Tiago's brows knitted together as he stared at her. "I assure you, our marriage is very real. Did you imagine there was some pretense in the proceedings?"

"It was more a figure of speech."

"I would never play games with something so critical," Tiago told her darkly.

"Because you're known for otherwise playing a great many games, of course," she said with a laugh.

And Lillie was not surprised that he did not laugh

with her. She wasn't sure why she was laughing herself, except she thought she was a bit more nervous than she wanted to let on. Because it was one thing to think about nights in Spain, and to make the best of things as she had been doing since, which had perhaps not been the hardship some people liked to think.

There was a part of her that mourned the loss of her solitary nights in her little room in Aberdeen, with the baby inside her and memories of Spain to keep her warm.

Because now the man in those memories was her *husband*, just as he would shortly become the *father* of their child—who she would no longer carry inside her—and maybe she wasn't quite as resigned to all of this change as she pretended.

This was all a little more disruption than she'd had planned when she'd taken Patricia's place at that resort.

It had certainly never occurred to her that if she did somehow find her mystery man one of these days, he would be so *stern*. So uncompromising, even though she was sure she could see little hints of that fearless, fiery lover she'd met that first night. But she supposed there was no crying over spilt milk. Not now.

She concentrated on the food instead, because she knew by now that it would be stellar, but as she was walking over to the table to take her seat, she stopped short. Her hands moved over her belly and she frowned.

Tiago was at her side in a moment, his hand on her elbow, his frown now an expression of concern. "Is something the matter?"

"I don't know…" Lillie murmured, because that fluttering sensation she'd felt off and on all day was back. But now it was more intense. And it didn't feel like a *jitter*, whatever that was.

Then it happened again, and she knew.

She looked up at him and did nothing at all to stop the delighted smile that moved over her face. She even laughed a little as the strangest feeling washed over her. A kind of relief, but far stronger than that, a kind of *marvel*.

That this was real, too. She was well and truly going to be a mother. She had made a baby who would grow up to be a *person*.

With this man beside her, who looked at her now as if he would tear apart the sky itself to keep her safe, if she only said the word.

It was like a different storm, brighter by far than any she'd known.

Lillie felt her smile becoming sappy at the edges, but she couldn't mind. She reached over and took his free hand and pulled it to her belly, holding it beneath hers so his palm was flush against her roundness.

And it came again, that fluttering.

"Is that…?" His voice sounded like she felt. The disbelief. The delight.

The wonder.

"It's the baby," she whispered, her eyes welling up a little. "The baby's kicking."

When he looked up at her again, she could see the emotion in those green-and-blue eyes, making them gleam like silver and gold besides.

"Our baby," he said thickly.

They were married. They were having this baby, together. *Ours*, he'd said.

Ours, she thought, like another vow.

"Yes," she said out loud, though her throat was tight. "Ours."

And Lillie understood for the first time just how much trouble she was in here. With Tiago, who looked at her in amazed wonder, his hands warm against the mound of her belly.

Because he would keep her safe, that she knew beyond any doubt.

But she wasn't sure she could say the same about her heart.

CHAPTER SIX

BY THE TIME the last month of this strange year began, Tiago felt certain he had everything in place. He had married Lillie and made certain she signed enough documents to keep his lawyers happy. He had secured his heir.

He had fixed the mistake he had made that heedless night in Spain, and he had made certain that kind of irresponsible recklessness would not be repeated.

"This is all irregular," the head of his legal team had tutted at him. "Normally we would never—"

"The Villela heir cannot be born out of wedlock," Tiago had replied, simply enough. "It simply is not done."

But he had carried that word like an indictment.

Because the man was not wrong. This was all highly irregular. And Tiago was not used to the sensation of finding himself in such a position. He had always done his duty. He had always made certain to handle each and every one of his responsibilities.

He did not make mistakes.

Lillie had been an anomaly from the start.

"I assume you roamed about Europe, hither and yon, conducting mad, passionate affairs wherever you went," she said one night at dinner.

Tiago had insisted on the same nightly meal that his parents had engaged in every single night of his childhood. When he had told them that his friends from boarding school did not spend their time eating with their families, his mother had scoffed.

Then they must not have much of a sense of their families, she had said. *But that will never be your fate,* meu filho.

Tonight, he questioned—not for the first time since he had brought Lillie home with him—what precisely he was thinking. He had spent the day in London, as he did often. It would have been easy enough to stay there, but then, it was not precisely a hardship to fly back to Portugal in the evening. He told himself that he was getting used to this routine, because he intended to be a presence in his child's life. He already knew how important that was.

But every time he thought about all the things he needed to put into place to raise a son or daughter the way he had been raised, he seemed to forget that Lillie was always a wildcard.

She wasn't even in her cups, as anyone else he knew would have had to be to carry on in such an indelicate manner, asking such impolitic questions.

By now he understood that this was simply Lillie.

"I beg your pardon," he said coolly. "I don't know what makes you think that I, Tiago Villela, would ever be so indiscriminate."

"Yes, what could possibly make me think that?" And in case he missed that she was being facetious, she let out that laugh of hers again. Speaking of indelicate things that he should probably attempt to curb, her laugh was a marvel of a thing. Husky and filled with light and merriment. There was something almost bawdy about it, and he told himself that it was more evidence that she was completely inappropriate in every possible way.

And yet, inappropriate or not, she was his wife.

"Is this your way of telling me that you have had many such nights yourself?" he asked, and was then appalled at himself. Men of gentility and breeding did not ask such questions. And he, personally, did not wish to know the answer. And more, did not wish to examine why he wished to protect himself from that knowledge.

"Certainly not." She wasn't looking at him. She was tucking into the local delicacies before her, with her usual deep and obvious relish for every bite. The spicy *franga da guia*, and *javali*, the wild boar that his people hunted on his own lands. And his favorite, *conquilhas à algarvia*, a mess of clams and garlic and coriander, cooked with savory Portuguese sausage and fried onions. He had not realized until

Lillie how many meals he'd sat through with women who did not like food. Or feared it. Women who had elaborate rituals and a great many rules.

Lillie simply ate her fill, and it was one of the most sensual things he had ever beheld.

"No?" he asked, perhaps too intently as he studied her. As if that might show him the fingerprints of her history all over her skin, little as he wished to see it.

She smiled at him in that guileless way she had that he could not understand. She was as free with a laugh as she was with a smile, and he couldn't make any sense of it. Tiago told himself he resented it, but that did not explain the hunger he felt for her, for her very presence, for the delight he took in what she would do or say next—

No, he corrected himself. *Delight* was not the right word. *Dismay* was much better. He was *dismayed* by her, obviously, because she was completely different from the sort of polished wife his parents had wanted for him.

The sort he had wanted for himself—someday far in the future.

Now he had to do his best to make *her* appropriate, because it was that or fight off this terrible *delight* that made him imagine he could be a different man. The kind of man he had been taught so clearly he could never, ever become.

Villelas were called to be better than that.

He had beaten back everything in him that was

different to make sure he not only heeded that call, but exemplified it.

It did not matter if he liked it. This was who he was.

But she was talking in that artless, appealing way of hers. "It might shock you to learn that I did not, in fact, indulge myself with a stable of European love interests to sustain me through the long Scottish winters."

"That resort has a reputation," he found himself saying, without meaning to. As if, in her presence, he was no longer the careful and considered man he was everywhere else. He could not account for it. "It is well known for fostering romantic interactions amongst the clientele."

"That would explain why my supervisor has always loved it so much," Lillie said. "She's told me many a time that she quite likes a drink and a shag of an evening." Her smile only deepened when she saw the frozen, appalled expression he could feel like a mask on his face. "I like to tell folks that I'm a bit of an acquired taste. By which I mean, I've always been cursed with standards."

"Standards are not a curse."

"Many of my housemates would disagree." Lillie picked up her glass and swirled the sparkling water she preferred at dinner around in it, her smile dimming— but only slightly. "I had a boyfriend my first two years of uni. He betrayed me, I'm afraid, and quite shockingly. There were scenes. It was ugly."

Once again, Tiago felt frozen, but for a much different reason. "What does that mean?"

"I caught him in the act," Lillie said simply, and while she wasn't smiling as she had before, she did not look devastated by the story she was telling. Was it time, he wondered? Had it dulled the sting? Or was it that it had been less devastating than dramatic even then? He couldn't know, but he could feel himself… thaw, slightly. "It was quite a palaver. I will admit that I was torn up at how *public* it all was for ages. Even though I knew that *of course* I was better off without the sort of person who would do such a thing, it took a long while for that to really sink in. And when it did, I found I was much less interested in being chatted up, or really having anything to do with a bloke on the pull. And then, somehow, years passed, and I didn't mind, but then I met a mysterious man who was not a pool boy in a Spanish resort."

She reached out and plucked up a plump shrimp from the platter that sat between them. With her fingers, which should have appalled him. He told himself that it did. That everything about her appalled him because it should have but instead, he found he was watching the way she popped the shrimp in her mouth, her lips closing over her own fingers—

He needed to stop.

"I'm sure your dating history is much more sophisticated and elegant," Lillie said. "Princesses and debutantes and endless galas, one can only assume."

"I have dated," he said, carefully. Even though *she* looked perfectly cheerful, as if unaware that this was a minefield. Because *he* certainly had not wished to hear about the uni boyfriend. The one he now felt the distinct urge to seek out, so he might mete out some overdue justice on Lillie's behalf. "But there is a very specific set of qualifications and attributes my future wife was meant to have, and I saw no need to get serious with anyone until I was ready to find the woman who exemplified that list."

"Oh, dear," Lillie said, those blue eyes of hers sparkly again. "I don't think I've ever *exemplified* a thing. Your poor list."

And when he thought about that later—after he'd left her there before dessert arrived, muttering something about a business call he did not have to make—what he remembered was how unconcerned she seemed. As if she truly did not care one way or the other about any list of attributes the wife of a Villela should have possessed.

She hadn't even asked what they were.

Tiago found himself brooding about them instead. And as the days passed, he cataloged Lillie's many flaws as he observed them, matching them against that list of spotlessness and sophistication in his head.

Especially when he was tempted to tell himself he didn't care about the discrepancy.

"You're doing it again," she said another night. This time, he had insisted they dress and eat in the elegant dining room. She sat to his right, and he expected that she would be overwhelmed by all the different plates and utensils that made up the sort of overly formal dinner he felt certain she had never indulged in before. But this was Lillie. She looked *entertained*, not overwhelmed. She even smiled at him now, her eyes dancing. "Looking at me and finding me wanting, at a guess."

That she could read him when no one else could made his skin feel too tight on his own body. "It is only that we will have to make certain that you receive the instruction you need," he told her stiffly. "There are certain expectations surrounding my name. I would hate for you to be out in the world and seen as a representative of this family without possessing the necessary skills, that's all."

"You are all heart, Tiago."

She said that serenely and then, holding his gaze in a manner he could only call challenging, she picked up the fork he had just been at pains to tell her was the wrong one, and used it anyway.

And later on, once again barricaded in his office—because he needed to leave her after these dinners where she sat about in pretty dresses, laughing and sparkling too brightly when the only thing that was meant to *sparkle* were the chandeliers—he thought about that list again. And more, about the way his parents had raised him.

They had made it perfectly clear what was expected of him.

Our family has too much wealth and power for you to expect that you should spend your life seeking happiness, his father had told him when he was a teenager. *You will hear many things as you grow, about how you must seek your truth. About how what truly matters is your own personal happiness. But the people who say these things are not Villelas.*

Yes, Pai, Tiago had replied when his father had leveled that familiar glare on him.

Villelas cannot be selfish. A Villela is more than welcome to seek contentment, Tiago, but happiness? His father had shaken his head. *It is better by far to strive for usefulness. You are a steward, not a star. This is what you must remember.*

Tiago had never forgotten.

Just as he never forgot being left when he'd dared *grieve* where they could see him.

Over time, there were more things he did not question. The way his parents always looked taken aback to see him, as if they'd forgotten all about him while he was off at school. The many holidays he and Leonor had been left to their own devices in one house or another, because his parents did not see any reason to curtail their schedules to see him.

The year that became two that he did not see them at all, because they had important things to see to elsewhere.

He had been ten, then eleven, and he had known better than to mention it when he saw them again.

Just as he knew, deep down, that all of this had made him stronger. More capable of doing what was necessary. More, that he needed it.

Because now he understood that he had a gift that most men of his wealth and consequence did not: he did not expect that he was the center of anyone's thoughts. He did not expect to be thought of at all.

It made him less arrogant—and more successful— than his peers.

He had never questioned what his parents had taught him, because he could see in everything he did that they had given him innumerable gifts. And he told himself he was not going to start questioning them now.

What he did question was how he was ever going to raise his own child with a woman who did not herself understand—or even *try* to understand—the realities of life as a Villela.

His parents had not loved each other. They would have recoiled at the very idea that they might. There were far more important things to concern themselves with, as they always made sure to tell him. They had always liked to say, quite proudly, that the vagaries of emotion were beneath them.

And his grandmother might have been a counterpoint to that in her time, but Tiago had only known her as a small boy. Small boys wanted to believe in all manner of impossible things. He felt grateful indeed that he had outgrown it.

He did not know why he did not tell Lillie these things.

Instead, he attempted to model his parents' relationship and modify Lillie's behavior as he went. Like the nightly dinners where he would ask her coolly what she did with her day, and, when she remembered to ask him the same, give her the concise and emotionless breakdown that he expected in return.

But though he realized this was how he expected colleagues to behave in business scenarios too, his wife did not seem to get the message.

"What exactly is the plan?" she asked one night.

He had spent the first part of their meal staring at her hair. She had caught the heavy mess of it up in the top of her head so there were riotous curls spilling out from what looked like a makeshift bun she had done herself. When he knew full well there was staff for such things, as he had hired them himself. She was a Villela wife now, and really, he ought to make it clear to her that she needed to think more elegance and less efficiency.

Yet somehow, he was too busy imagining wrapping his fingers in those curls to say anything about how she'd styled them tonight. "At the moment, the plan is to have a quiet, congenial dinner and an early night, as my presence is required in London in the morning."

"I mean for me," she said. "I can't say I minded being on a bit of a holiday from the real world, but surely I'll need to *do* something. I can't drift about the house all day long, can I?" She sighed. "I need a job, Tiago."

He blinked at that, letting the sheer temerity of it settle. A bit. "Villela wives do not work."

Lillie propped her chin on one hand. "What did your mother do with her days?"

Tiago sat back in his chair. "She had a great many interests. Her family had once been deeply involved in the cork industry here, and she was instrumental in the founding of a local museum that explores the impact of cork not only on this region, but on Portugal as a whole. Her other charitable interests included literacy, medical conditions that were dear to her heart for any number of sad reasons, and she also bred her hounds. Podengos."

"None of that sounds like a job."

"Lillie." He shook his head, taken back. "You cannot *work*, of course."

"You make that sound dirty. *Working.* When you do it yourself."

"Villela wives do not," he replied. And he sighed when she stared back at him in a kind of amazement.

"It isn't done. I understand that you came into this accidentally, Lillie. That can't be helped. I'm willing to make allowances."

She laughed, but somehow, it was less merry than usual. "Allowances?"

"The ideal wife for a man in my position would have been trained from birth to assume this role. Part of the training would include being an heiress of great rank and fortune herself. She would have been educated in the finest schools and would have involved herself in only the most worthy charities afterward. There would never be any question of her *working* in some menial job."

"It is a terrible pity, then, you could not have married this paragon." Lillie gazed at him as if she pitied him. But also, if he wasn't mistaken, as if she wanted to take the fork she held and throw it at him. "What a shame it is that you have been saddled with the likes of me, a peasant straight through. Why, I don't know how you can hold your head up."

"I didn't offer any moral judgments," he said, and it was distressing to find that he had to work to keep his voice steady. Calm. To remain the man he had worked so hard to become, and not give in to the strange urges this woman brought out in him.

"Didn't you?" she asked. She pushed back at the table and stood up too quickly, and he shot to his feet, too. Without knowing he meant to move.

"Villelas do not make scenes in the middle of a

meal," he told her, a bit more darkly than was wise. He knew it even as he said it. "Or at all."

Lillie glared at him. "Villelas can do whatever they like, with my blessing, but I am a grown woman who will continue to do as she likes. What I'm trying to tell you, Tiago, is that I'm bored."

"Bored." He repeated the word as if it was a curse. Because, to him, it always had been. His parents had made sure of that.

"Bored silly," she shot right back at him. "I've taken a thousand walks. I've read stacks and stacks of books. I've entertained myself by asking your staff for outrageous things to see if they can provide them on a moment's notice, and guess what? They can. If this is the life of the rich and famous, I'm sorry to tell you it's tedious in the extreme."

"There are many people who would kill to have these advantages you consider so boring."

"It's not the advantages that I don't like," she fired back. "It's that I need a purpose. Surely you understand that. You seem to have such an ingrained idea of what your life is meant to be. You know your purpose here. But what's mine? Given that I'm not this perfect, effortlessly aristocratic Villela wife of myth and legend. I need to do *something* or I'll go mad."

"You are my wife. You will be the mother of my child." He very nearly laughed, not that he found this amusing. "It seems to me that should be enough to occupy your thoughts instead of all these unnecessary concerns about some outside purpose."

"Oh," Lillie said sweetly, "you are my husband and will be the father of this child. Does it consume *your* thoughts?"

He thought he might actually have growled. "I think of little else."

She blew out a breath. "The baby is going to come one way or another. And like it or not, I will have to figure out how to be a mother then." She shook her head. "In the meantime, I'm a wife, but I don't even know what that means. And I don't think you do, either."

"I know exactly what a Villela wife must be," he retorted. "As I have been at pains to tell you. My mother was remarkably good at it. After she died, my father told anyone who would listen that there is no point in him remarrying, because no one else could possibly do it as well as she did."

"Do what?" Lillie asked, very distinctly, as if he was the one being obtuse.

"She supported him in all things. Everything she did, everything she said, brought honor to our name."

"But what about their marriage?" Lillie demanded. "Did they laugh? Did they play games? You never say what they were *like*. Did they kick off their shoes and dance around this table? Did they fight, have private jokes, and hold hands on their afternoon walks?"

Tiago stared at her in astonishment. "I don't have

the slightest idea what you're talking about. They worked well together. They were an excellent team."

"Did they *like* each other?" Lillie asked, throwing her hands wide.

"Do yours?" And it was exactly the sort of ill-measured, ill-considered retort that he knew better than to make. What was it that this woman did to him?

She crossed her arms then and tipped up her chin, glowering at him as if this was some kind of altercation. When Tiago did not have altercations. "They do all of those things. My parents met when they were children. They grew up in the same village. They were each other's first…everything. They've been wildly in love with each other and the very best of friends as long as either one of them can remember."

Tiago could not have said why he felt so…unnerved by this revelation. And almost embarrassed, as if this was not the sort of thing that ought to be discussed in polite company.

"That's very nice for them, I'm sure."

"It's not always nice at all," Lillie shot back. "They love me, don't get me wrong, but they love each other more. Sometimes, growing up, I felt a bit like a third wheel. I always suspected the real reason they didn't have more children is because they preferred not to divert much more of their attention from each other. And then there was the impossibility of living up to a love like that. I suspect that half the reason I felt so wrecked by my university boy-friend's behavior was that I had to tell my parents that I wasn't like them after all."

"My parents never pretended to be in love," Tiago said, and he could not understand why he felt on the defensive. "They would have been horrified if anyone suggested that they should succumb to such mawkishness."

And he had closed the distance between them again, when he knew better. When he knew, in fact, that it was the last thing he should allow. Yet there he was, so close that if he'd wanted, he could have reached out and touched her—but he didn't.

Lillie's eyes were too big, too blue. "That's one of the saddest things I've ever heard."

"You don't understand." He wanted to rake his hands through his hair, but he did not *fidget* like a child. Tiago blew out a breath. "That's my fault, not yours. I clearly have not adequately explained to you the weight of the responsibilities that both of my parents carried, and that you and I must carry as well. There is no space for any of these things that you've been talking about here. There is only duty. Responsibility. And the contentment that those things can bring."

"That," Lillie said, very distinctly, with what could only be called the light of battle in her blue eyes, "sounds like a terribly sad life, Tiago."

He leaned closer, just slightly. Just to make his point. "You don't know what you're talking about."

"What I know is that what you're describing sounds like a long, slow, frigid death," she shot back, something like passion—or fear—in her voice. He didn't like either. "I want no part of that. I've been close enough to it myself and I don't want to go back. I don't want all that numbness and banging on about *responsibilities*. Responsibilities are there no matter what, aren't they? I want to feel *alive*."

And then, as if that wasn't outrageous enough, she closed the distance between them, shot up on her toes, and kissed him.

CHAPTER SEVEN

LILLIE WISHED SHE'D thought to kiss him sooner, rather than daintily waiting for *him* to kiss *her*.

That was the only thought that worked its way through her as she stood there, her mouth on his at last, no longer quite so concerned with boredom. Or purpose. Or long, slow slides into a walking death, all in the name of the family honor. Whatever *that* was when it was at home.

This had been the answer all along.

This was what she should have done the moment she'd walked into his office, to remind them both that this lightning bolt was what had brought them together and everything else was secondary to that.

This felt as right tonight as it had that night in Spain.

And what she felt, first and foremost, was relief.

He was still *him*. They were still *them*.

This was still real.

So she just kept right on kissing him.

Lillie kissed him until he made a low sound, like a growl, in the back of his throat. She kissed him until his hands came to her face, then traveled over the rest of her. He trailed fire and need down her back, her upper thighs. He found her breasts, moved over her belly, and then his palms gripped her bottom.

And still the kiss went on and on.

Though there was nothing the slightest bit *frigid* about it.

"What are you doing to me?" he grated out, tearing his lips from hers for the barest second.

"Doing something," she whispered back, "about this terrible boredom."

And then she laughed, because he swept her up into his arms. It shouldn't have worked. He should have staggered under the weight of her, because she was big and round these days and she had never been an airy little thing in the first place.

But Tiago did not seem to notice. He hoisted her high against his chest, and gazed down at her in a way that made her shiver.

Because she knew this look. She knew this man. She even knew why he carried her like this, the way he had back in Spain that night because he did not want to part with her for even as long as it would take for her to walk from one part of her room to the other.

Like then, he kept stopping so he could kiss her again.

Deeper. Hotter.

With all those storms she could see in his eyes.

And she knew that this had been building for too long. Since Spain, maybe. And ever since the wedding, she had been waiting for him to do something about it, but that was foolish. Left to his own devices, Tiago would sit about in stiff-looking suits, droning on about duty and honor until she wanted to start throwing the crockery about, just to make *something* happen.

Note to self, she thought as he carried her down one hallway, then up a set of stairs, not seeming to even breathe heavily while he did it. *Kiss the man. As often as possible. So he is not tempted to forget that this is how we got into this mess in the first place.*

It was one thing to ponder that particular mess while sitting on her own, yet again, in her guest suite. It was one thing to brood on it as she walked out into the vineyards, alone.

Revisiting that mess, with all the heat and wonder that had caused it in the first place... Well. That was something else.

Lillie pulled him down with her when he laid her out so carefully on a big, wide bed in what she took to be his bedchamber.

And later she might think more about the fact that it seemed so stark in here, so austere, that it reminded her of a monastery. More like a hotel suite than a man's personal bedchamber, but she couldn't care about that. Not now.

Not when he was finally stretched out beside her once again.

Lillie accepted, in that moment, that she'd thought this would never happen again. She'd thought it and she would have said that she'd come to terms with it, too. Because what choice did she have? She had first tried to find him, but had been forced to give up on it. And woven into all the ways she'd thought about the fact that she was set to become a single mother had been that secret bit of sadness she hadn't known how to share. Not with herself. Not with anyone.

She'd missed him. She'd missed this.

And there was no possible way to explain that to anyone.

Because it was only one night. That was all they'd shared. It shouldn't have meant anything.

But that had always been the trouble with Tiago.

She knew, and she thought he knew too, that everything had changed when they'd laid eyes on each other. That kind of thing was supposed to be a myth. It wasn't supposed to be possible. If asked, she would have told anyone who would listen to her that love at first sight wasn't real. Even her own parents, still in love to this day, hadn't had that. Theirs was a love that had grown deeper and richer over time, as they liked to tell anyone who would listen.

But that didn't change the fact that Lillie had looked up, seen Tiago, and everything after that had felt…inevitable.

It still did.

He was muttering words she didn't understand now, pressing them into her skin as he moved over her, kissing her as he went.

And there was no time for this. There was no *time* because there had been nothing but time and she couldn't bear it. Lillie couldn't keep her hands to herself. She pulled at his clothes, pushing his hands away when he got in her way. She was in a kind of panic, so desperate to get her hands on his bare skin. To get her mouth into the crook of his neck. To rediscover that astonishing V carved above his hips.

To learn him all over again, like this was new.

But before she came anywhere near getting her fill, he was rolling her over again. He put her on her back so he could peel her dress from her body, make short work of her undergarments, and then settle there beside her so he could finally learn this new shape of her.

And he dedicated himself to the task.

He ordered her to lie still when she wanted to fight him, because she wanted to rise up and wrap herself around him. She wanted to reacquaint herself with him, too. She wanted to feel him everywhere, real skin to real skin, not the dreams she'd been surviving on all this time.

"My poor, greedy *benzinho*," he murmured, that current of laughter back in his voice.

At last.

It wasn't there when he told her what Villelas did and didn't do, as if he couldn't decide to change it if he liked. It wasn't there when he lectured her on duty and told her about the perfect wife he hadn't married.

It was only here, with his mouth against her skin and his hands moving from her tender breasts down the length of her body. Here where he lingered over her bump, then found his way to the oversensitized furrow where she longed for him most. It was only here, she thought, that he was truly himself.

That he was actually alive.

But she knew better than to say it.

"Why aren't you inside me?" she demanded instead.

Because she wanted him there, but also because she wanted the dark velvet of his laugh. The rumble of it, whisking over her skin and then into her, too, even before he pressed his long, strong fingers deep into her soft heat.

Even before he made her sigh, then moan.

As she rose, pressing her hips up to meet him, he began to move his fingers in and out of her, so slowly she didn't know if she wanted to scream or cry.

So instead of making such impossible choices, Lillie did both at the same time.

And it seemed as if an eternity crept by with her strung out there, stretched between the two, lost in the sheer perfection of his touch. Lost in how well he seemed to understand each and every one of her body's responses. He anticipated them. He worked her toward them, then through them.

Over and over again.

It seemed as if there was nothing to do but surrender to such mastery, so that was what she did.

And Tiago, gentleman that he was, gave her a great many opportunities to get it right.

Then, when she was reduced to nothing but a shivering, shuddering mess of sensation and need and desire, he rolled her over to settle her astride him.

He slid his hands to her hips. And his gaze was a storm, deep blues and complicated greens.

"I do not know how different this will be for you," he said, his voice gruff and low.

A warning, maybe. Or a statement of intent. Either way, the shiver that moved over her was made entirely of delight.

Even though Lillie thought that there ought to be something wrong with this. In kneeling there as she was, her knees spread wide on either side of him and that great, thick length of him standing up between them. Standing up and rubbing gently against the swell of her belly. Where their baby grew, even now.

She thought it shouldn't be sensual, but it was. Because he and she had come together just like this to make this baby in the first place. They had done all of this together, just like this.

And that they were together again, naked and wild-eyed and filled once more with all this heat and light, felt like magic. Like a miracle.

Lillie thought this was the season for it, anyway.

And then shuddered again when he smoothed his hands over her bump, as if he felt it, too. The sweet joy that they were married. The particular glory of the fact that the wildfire, astonishing connection between them had made a person. A person that they would meet in a couple of months.

The wonder of all of this—of everything that had come from their gazes clashing together in Spain. Of all that would come, stretching on far into the future.

She thought she ought to have felt dizzy, but that wasn't it. Not quite.

"I have no idea how it will feel," she told Tiago.

And then watched as a smile moved over his face.

Because this was the only way Tiago Villela smiled, as far as she knew. Naked and in bed—and wickedly.

"We will discover it together, you and I," he promised her.

And then his hands moved to her hips. It occurred to her that she had essentially told him that she'd been with no one since him, and even though that was no more than the truth, she couldn't help but think that put her at some kind of disadvantage—

But then there was no point thinking about advantages or disadvantages, because there was only feeling.

There was only this.

There was only him.

Because his hard hands moved her until she was

kneeling up, then moving so she could press down on that thick, hard length of him.

And it was…different. He felt bigger, harder. She was so sensitive, so new.

Or maybe it was because he lay there beneath her, watching her closely with those glorious eyes gleaming darkly, and once he had her positioned the way he wanted, he…took his time.

First he played a bit at her entrance, and then, when she shook and sobbed and cursed his name, he laughed. Then he eased himself inside, only slightly. Only a little, then pulled back out.

Then he did it again.

And again.

Then, with that iron clasp on her hips that prevented her from doing anything but giving herself over into his hands, he eased in just the faintest little bit more, then back out.

And he seemed perfectly content to continue doing exactly that. Moving into her a little more each time, but only in the tiniest increments.

But so slowly.

So terribly, wonderfully slowly and with such perfect control that it made Lillie almost embarrassingly aware of how out of control she was. Outside herself, turned inside out.

At points she tried to fight, but it was no use. He would not let her simply sink down and take all of him. He would not let her control a thing.

Instead, he murmured words of encouragement in several languages. He made that low, growling sort of noise that seemed to set each and every one of her nerve endings on fire.

His voice was a kind of husky croon, its own sensual bombardment.

Lillie found herself with her head thrown back, her hair everywhere, her back arched so intensely it should have hurt.

And it was possible it took whole lifetimes before he finally lowered her all the way down, so that he was embedded inside her as deep as he could go.

Once he did, she could do nothing but pant as she opened her eyes and stared down at him. Not sure if she wanted to kiss him or kill him as she trembled, still held fast in between his hands.

Again, that smile of his moved over his stern face. He lifted her up and she almost cried, thinking he was starting the whole process over again—

But instead, Tiago thrust up into her and brought her down hard to meet him, and it was like everything before was thunder, but this—

This was the lightning.

It hit her, she ignited, and then she splintered into too many pieces to ever fully recover.

She shook and shook. She rocked against him, sobbing out the white-hot, overwhelming pleasure of this. Of him.

Tiago moved beneath her, but only enough to keep

her going and going, dancing in the flames, shaking and sobbing.

Until finally she was limp and dazed, and so he sat up. Staying deep inside her, he pulled her against his chest and began to move her that way.

And once again, every thrust was a revelation.

Lillie was oversensitive, or maybe it was just him, but all she could seem to do was burst into flames. Again and again, one time barreling straight into the next. He wrapped his arms around her back, so that all she had to do was meet his thrusts as best she could—

Because it was all too much. And it was nowhere near enough. It felt brand-new and as if she'd finally come home.

She lost count of the times she shivered and sobbed her way over that cliff. Each time was infused with that lightning and as much of a glorious shock as the first. He made her fall apart with her hands sunk deep in his hair, and his in hers, that tiny stinging, making it better. Different.

Another time, she was kissing him hungrily, deeply. So that he was inside her in two places, her nipples rubbing against his chest, so she simply imploded there, unable to do anything at all but let it happen.

Again and again she caught fire and each and every time, he caught her as she came down and threw her straight back up again.

Demonstrating all the while that iron control that she'd thought about far too many times over the past months. And thinking about it now, while experiencing it again, had predictable results. Because the harder he was inside her, the more the intensity of the way he held himself back made his eyes dark and gleaming, the softer she was. The hotter she was.

And the wilder it was when she broke apart.

Until finally his whole body tightened, and he grew stiffer inside her. He reached up to put his hands on her face, so they were gazing at each other once more, both of them flushed. Both of them chiseled bare at the overwhelming magic of this thing between them.

Raw, she thought. *Mine.*

"Hold on," Tiago ordered her darkly.

"I always do," she whispered back.

Maybe what she meant was, *I always will*. Maybe that was what he heard.

Because he bared his teeth, those maddeningly steady thrusts inside her grew wild and erratic, and this time, it was the scalding heat of him inside her as he roared out his release that sent her over the edge, chasing after him, tumbling over and over and into the stars beside him.

And it seemed as if a great many years had passed by the time she woke up again to find herself curled up at his side. Though he had clearly gotten up in the meantime. The fire danced in the grate, warming the room. And he had pulled a throw over her, as she rested her head upon him like a pillow.

He was his own furnace. She remembered that, too. And she was a Scottish girl, always cold. A man who burned like Tiago did made her feel nothing but safe, warm, and cared for.

Even though she felt as if she was moving through a fog just now, she knew better than to say that. She smiled sleepily at him, finding his gaze in the fire-light.

Tiago looked…brooding, if anything. But he did not speak. He reached over and dragged his thumb over her lips, then ran his palm over whatever shape her curls had made.

"Tiago," she began.

"I sent for food," he told her curtly. "As I expect you will be hungry."

And she hadn't been a moment ago, but the minute he said it, food was all she could think about. He rolled to the edge of the bed and she followed him, accepting the whisper-soft wrapper he handed her, like a caress against her bare skin.

Then she sat with him in front of the fire, only too happy to tuck into the platters of food that waited there. Cheeses and meats, warm breads and pots of sweet butter. She was thirsty too, and drank deep, and it was only when she sat back and sighed a little that Tiago made that low, growling noise again that made her shiver all over again.

And then she forgot all about the food, because he was moving over her. He shifted her into place beneath him on a soft leather couch, then shouldered her thighs apart, settling himself there between her legs so he could eat her up, like dessert.

After he got her screaming and falling apart all over again, he lifted her up and carried her with him into a bathroom suite even more impressive than hers. He took her into what seemed to be a large tiled room, but turned out to be as big a shower as she'd ever seen, with sprays of water coming from all sides.

Tiago had her again there, holding her up against the warm walls and letting the water pound down all around them until they both burned too bright to bear.

And it reminded her so much of Spain. It had been like this then, too.

Every touch seemed endless. Every spark a whole bonfire.

It had been an eternity, that night. Maybe only one night had passed outside her hotel room, but inside it, there had been this. A deep knowing she never could have explained to anyone. A recognition.

An eternity.

And now it was threaded through with so many more layers. The baby. Their wedding, however businesslike.

The lifetime she'd felt with him that night, stretching out in front of them.

And she slept so deeply beside him that she shouldn't have been able to wake, but she did—to find his mouth wicked temptation, teasing her back into that wicked dance again and again all night, as if all of this was new.

As if none of it could last, just like before.

But this time, she told herself dreamily, she would not wake alone. This time, she knew his name. She would not spend months without him.

She could see the smudge of a new day's light outside his windows when she woke for the last time that night. And this time it was slow.

An inexorable unraveling, not a bright lightning strike.

And maybe all the more unsettling because of it.

Lillie felt undone, unspooled. She shuddered against him. His head tipped into the crook of her neck, and they shook together, there in what was left of the dark.

Leaving them raw.

Bare.

Seen, she thought as she drifted off to sleep once more.

When she woke the next time, the sun was pouring in from outside and she was alone in his bed.

Lillie didn't really like how that felt, but this wasn't Spain. For one thing, she was already pregnant.

As she swung out of the bed, she told herself all the rest of the ways this was different. She knew his name. She supposed she'd taken his name, though for all his talk of *Villela wives*, she hadn't given any particular thought to keeping her name or taking his. Still, she was in his bedroom, not some random hotel room.

"This isn't the same thing at all," she told herself briskly.

She went to use his shower, though she was half-afraid of drowning herself in all those different sprays. When she came out, there were new clothes waiting for her on the bed she'd left a mess that was already made.

They were like ghosts, these servants of his, and she wasn't sure she would ever get used to it. But she still pulled on the outfit someone else had picked out for her. And like all the clothes that had been provided for her here, it was a lesson in simplicity. Another one of those shockingly comfortable T-shirts that bore no resemblance to any T-shirts she had ever worn in her life. A pair of jeans that were softer still, but the stretchy waistband that not only fit her belly, it made her feel supported. Not simply bloated and round, but a woman with a figure.

She pulled on the sweater they'd left for her, too, a simple crewneck thing, except it, too, felt like soft, sweet dreams as it fell into place against her body. And when she glanced in the nearest mirror, she laughed, because she looked well classy in a way she never had before.

Who knew that all it took was posh clothes, well cut.

Something about that made her laugh again, though it didn't quite take away from that clutching sense of uncertainty deep inside.

And Lillie didn't like that at all, so she set out to find him, only realizing as her toes got cold that she'd neglected to stamp her feet into the boots they'd left next to the bed. Meaning she was padding around the gaspingly fancy house in her bare feet, which she did not have to consult Tiago to know was not how a Villela wife was meant to comport herself.

She chose to take that as a good sign. Because the last thing she wanted was to live her life in that kind of coma. Everything he'd ever said about his parents made her stomach hurt.

Lillie went to his study first, but he wasn't there. She had thought that study of his was his office, but it was only in exploring the house in her bare feet and morning-after hair that she came across him in a modernized office space tucked away on the floor below his bedroom. When she peered in, he was on a video chat of some kind, nodding with ill-concealed impatience as people spoke to him rapidly in different languages.

When he replied, it was as calm and stern as ever, and Lillie couldn't tell if her reaction was a sweet joy or a kind of deep consternation—but either way, it made her flush.

When the call ended, he turned from the desk

where he'd been standing, arms folded, frowning into the screen on the far wall.

She'd been uneasy since she woke up. A little dismayed, even, that he'd repeated his original disappearing act. But the whole time, she'd told herself it was a hangover from Spain. That everything was different now.

She'd counted all the ways.

But all it took was one look now, and Lillie knew she been right to worry.

Because her husband looked straight through her, long and slow and frigid, as if she was a stranger.

CHAPTER EIGHT

THE DECEMBER DAYS rolled along and it was as if Lillie had somehow found herself married to two husbands instead of one.

It would have been panic-inducing, if she let it.

Every night was a mad, intense exploration of each other. Just like Spain had been. Only this wasn't one night in Spain followed by five months of longing. This was better, because it was deeper.

Because they knew each other now. They knew each other better every day. And every night their bodies sang out in recognition of that ongoing intimacy. What had struck them both like lightning at that resort became hotter because it was deeper now. Because of the things they shared. The baby they were expecting. The house they lived in. The interactions they had that brought them inexorably closer, like it or not, and then set them alight in the dark.

Every night was better than the night before. Every night seemed longer, more shattering. They turned to each other in that bed again and again, but no matter how endless and devastatingly *good* it all was, one thing held true.

Every morning Tiago would wake up and act as if none of that had ever happened.

As if he had actually kept his promise that he would never touch her again.

He became that stranger, and Lillie had to fight to keep her panic to herself, because she wanted the man she knew. The man she had clapped eyes on back in Spain and had longed for ever since.

Not this ice sculpture who made her worry that she was slowly freezing over herself.

Daytime Tiago was all business and frigid straight through, and while he did not look at her as if she was a *stranger* necessarily, he maintained a certain chilly distance.

"I cannot countenance boredom," he told her that first morning, when she'd gone to find him in her bare feet and had found him as shut down as she'd ever seen him. "So I've taken the liberty of making sure that tedium does not overtake you while, at the same time, directing your considerable energy in a more appropriate direction."

"That sounds a bit boring, actually," she replied, mostly to see him glower, but also to cover up the panicked catapulting of her pulse at the sight of him like this. "Who fancies being *directed* anywhere, much less somewhere *appropriate*?"

But the Tiago she was married to by day did not react the way she knew he would at night. He did not even sigh, though his expression suggested that he might. Internally. And what Lillie learned that day was that when Tiago *took the liberty*, as he put it, what he was actually doing was laying down the law. Arranging his world in the manner he saw fit. Whether it was providing her with a wardrobe that matched his sensibilities or filling her days with lessons.

Lillie was tempted to complain, but the truth was, she'd always loved school. Private tutoring was even better, as it allowed her to go at her own pace without having to slow down for anyone else. Tiago started her off with Portuguese and Spanish lessons in language and history, because, he told her, the child would certainly speak both fluently.

"You can be sure the bairn will speak English as well as Scots, then, too," Lillie replied when he made one of his decrees about their child's future fluency, as if he was handing down stone tablets from on high. "Shall I get you a tutor? *Chan eil aon chànan gu leòr.*"

But it was daytime Tiago she was telling that one language was not enough, so all he did was gaze at her in that way of his. It suggested the imminent possibility of disappointment and more forbearance than ought to be required.

Tiago by day was a frustration in male form, Lillie

often thought in the weeks that followed. Panic lurked in their every interaction, because how could she stay married to a man so cold? How could she let him raise her child?

She couldn't answer that to her satisfaction. But she wasn't the slightest bit bored.

In addition to her language and history classes, she received lessons in comportment so that her sometimes-elegant appearance could be matched by a host of elegant actions. Or in any case, that was what the tiny woman dressed in an ever-changing array of chic scarves worn with notable aplomb informed her.

With enough hauteur that made it clear that *her* elegance was innate, not taught.

"I don't quite see the point polishing up this particular sow's ear into any kind of silk purse," Lillie said chattily at one of the stiff dinners Tiago insisted upon, this one after a day of lessons on cutlery. "What does it matter?"

"It only matters if you plan to go out in polite company at some point," Tiago said in that *I am the Villela heir* voice of his, all steel and certainty. "I assumed you would not wish to embarrass your own child, who, make no mistake, will be raised with all the manners incumbent upon his or her station."

Lillie poked at the salted cod before her. It appeared in some form or another at every meal, because it was the national dish of Portugal, according to Leonor. And Lillie was a proper Scottish woman who might prefer haddock from her local chippy, but she had never met a piece of fish she didn't like. The infinite variations of *bacalhau* pleased her immensely.

But tonight what she liked most was stabbing at it. "This is a very special talent you have, Tiago. To already be using our child as a bargaining chip when it hasn't even been born yet."

"I will never *use* our child," he replied in a low voice, with an intensity that made her sit a little straighter, so much did it remind her of the man she met only in their bed when the moon was high, almost like he wished he was still nothing more than a dream she had. "What I will do is protect that child, just as I will protect you, even if what I must protect you both from is you."

He delivered that last bit in faintly ringing tones. Lillie stopped abusing the poor meal before her. She sat back in her seat and eyed him for a moment. "And who will protect you?" she asked.

She didn't add, *from yourself.*

But he didn't answer anyway.

Because he insisted that they spend the whole of the evening meal in the very stiff and formal manner he felt was appropriate. That was how his parents had raised him, and he made it clear each night that he thought they'd had the right of it.

And she wanted to flip the table when the panic

got into her bones, but she didn't. She went along with it, because she knew that after dinner there were drinks. Because that was also what civilized people did, apparently. They very theatrically rose from the table and moved to a drawing room or study—likely because they had houses with so many rooms and needed to use them all. Once in the chosen second location, they sat and had further conversations, though more casually, and it was only then that the Tiago she preferred emerged.

Every evening, when he came back to her, the relief just about bowled her over.

Lillie would have been happy if the nights went on forever. It was the endless days that made her wonder if she was going mad. Or if she'd stumbled into one of her favorite torrid novels where a woman found herself married off to a grim man in some castle somewhere, only to discover the passionate lover he only became in the dark was his disgraced twin. Or a vampire, she wasn't picky.

She wasn't picky about Tiago by night, either. She tried to enjoy him as fully as she could, and warm herself in all that fire of his, because she knew it would be chilly again come morning.

But there was less time to puzzle over the mysteries of the two sides of Tiago when he added to her lessons halfway through December. This time, it wasn't more attempts to make up for her lack of a debutante ball, it was classes on finance. Business. Wealth management and estate planning.

"Dare I hope that it's your intention to add me to your company roster?" she asked one afternoon as they were coming up fast on the bleak midwinter. Not, of course, that there was anything particularly bleak about the Algarve at this time of year, though the locals complained about the cooler weather and the clouds. Facetiously, to her mind. All Lillie saw was the light.

Nighttime Tiago might laugh a little when she said things like that, and scrape his teeth along the line of her neck as punctuation, en route to driving them both wild. The daytime version only gazed at her, making a bit of a show of that faint frown between his eyes.

"I was unaware that you wish to interview for a position in my company," he replied, with that coolness that she believed was *meant* to make her wither where she stood. Which was only one of the reasons she did not. "Competition is fierce and the process is considered grueling."

"I assumed that was why you added all those new classes," she said, fighting the panic within at the slap of chilliness from him. She tried her best to meet it with a certain…languid unconcern, whether she felt it or not. She'd taken to invading his office for a cup of tea in the afternoon, as that was what *she* considered behavior appropriate to her people. And tried to act as she meant to go on. As if he was the husband she wanted, not the one he played by day. As if she could make him see, somehow, that it was better when he was. As if this might all work out, somehow, instead of stranding her and her baby on this relentless glacier he liked so much. It was more of an effort every day. "I'm becoming quite an expert on financial matters and the business affairs of the landed gentry. I thought perhaps you were planning to make me your new chief financial officer or the like."

Lillie thought nothing of the kind, but it was amusing to claim otherwise. Because he would draw himself up in all his offended dignity and try to invoke a blizzard or two with his freezing tones, and she would smile innocently back at him and wait for sundown, when he usually readdressed the outrageous things she'd done in the light. Deliciously.

That part of this game she liked.

It was better than driving herself mad with the increasing fear that she was going to be stuck here, and not with the man she wanted. And how would she keep her child from withering in this terrible, endless winter?

Lillie tried her best not to think of it, and, therefore, thought of very little else.

"In a manner of speaking," Tiago said. And when he looked at her then, he was expressionless, but there was something about that dark gleam in his gaze that made her sit straighter in the chair. Usually she preferred to lounge about in complete defiance of everything her tiny dictator demanded she do in her comportment classes. "You are my wife now."

"In more ways than one," she agreed, and then beamed at him when his gaze narrowed. Because he did not like to be reminded that he was not maintaining the boundaries he'd set down long since.

Tiago had been perfectly clear about that in those first few days, when it became clear that he could not stay away from her at night and more, that he hated himself for it in the morning. At first Lillie felt almost complimented. She had never been the sort of woman who inspired such strong reactions in anyone. Certainly not in men.

But she felt significantly less complimented as time went on. And had got a bit salty about it in turn.

Because the salt covered up what she knew—that this couldn't last. That at least one of them would break, and she was horribly worried it was going to be her.

If I could control myself, benzinho, *I would*, he had growled at her, backing her across the length of the small study that second evening, after such a long, cold day. Because it was dark outside, and as she was about to discover, he was his very own kind of werewolf. *If I could keep my hands off you, I would. And believe me, the day will come when I will make certain that we behave appropriately. The way we should have been doing all along.*

What does appropriate *even mean between us?* she had dared ask him. *Everything that happened has been anything but.*

But we are both Villelas now, he had growled, coming to a stop there before the bookcase once he had backed her as far as she could go. He had placed a hand on either side of her and leaned in so she could see the blaze of fire in him. The intoxicating heat, just there, shimmering in all that blue and green. *And Villelas have standards.*

As it happens, she'd whispered, lifting her chin, *I haven't decided whether or not I'm taking your name.*

Though she had certainly called it out a lot that night, both there in the study and upstairs in his bed, until the dawn turned him to ice again.

But she did not think that was what he was thinking about as he stared at her now, forbiddingly, across the expanse of his very important desk.

"You are my wife," he said the way he often did, making sure she could see how he had to call upon his patience. "And it is entirely possible that I might die before you. I would hate to imagine you adrift after I'm gone, a target for disreputable people. It would be far better if you were capable of stepping in and controlling my estate yourself. It's only rational."

But there was something about the way he tacked

that last part on, she thought. As if it had only occurred to him just then that he could use that as an
excuse.

And as she stared back at him, that gaze of his
changed. It became...less cool.

Lillie did not pretend that she didn't know that
no matter what he said, or how he dressed it up and
tried to make it matter-of-fact, he was giving her a
compliment. More than that.

Because his responsibilities, his duties, were the
most important thing in the world to him. And if it
was her opinion that he clung to them like a drowning man, desperately reaching out for any bits of
floating debris to call a life preserver, she wisely
kept that to herself.

At least by day.

"If it's up to me," she said, aware that her voice
was hushed, then, "I'd prefer it if you lived."

And she knew she wasn't wrong about the way he
looked back at her, hushed himself, as if all of this
was a sacred moment. And more, that he might not
have intended it that way. That he might have con-
vinced himself that it was, indeed, only a purely rational move that had to do with the estate, not her.

But their eyes locked in that way that had always
been almost too honest to bear. And Lillie knew, the
way she always knew, that they both knew the truth.

She also knew he didn't like it.

"Time is not granted to us," he gritted out after

a long moment. "If it was, my parents would have lived forever. They might not have loved each other, not in the way you insist your parents do. But they loved what they built. They loved the history of their great families and the legacies that made them who they were. If it was up to them, they never would have left those things behind."

"And what of you, Tiago?" she dared ask, though her ribs seemed to clamp down hard against her heart. "Surely they loved you?"

He looked almost stricken for a moment. Then he looked down and she saw his mouth curve, though it was no smile.

"As I said," and it took him a moment to raise his gaze to hers again, she thought, and a moment more to keep his gaze so clear, so fiercely steady, "they were both deeply enamored of their legacies."

She slid a hand over her belly and pressed her fingers in to meet tiny kicks that greeted her. And silently she vowed, *I will never be enamored of you, my wee sweet bairn. I will love you madly all the days of my life.*

But Tiago continued to look at her in that almost-stricken manner from behind his desk, and she felt a sharp stab of pain—for him. For the man who had been left to stand here behind an uncaring desk, talking of legacies when what he patently needed was love.

And she knew he would never ask for something

he wanted. She doubted he knew how. So she held his gaze, and kept hers solemn. Befitting the solemnity of this occasion, even though she knew he would deny it was happening even now. Even though he would argue to the death that it made sense, that was all.

"Thank you," she said. Very carefully. Very deliberately. "It will be an honor, though I hope I'm never called upon to do it."

And that night, he was like a man unleashed and untamed, raw and wild.

As if both of them were more naked than ever before, more connected and more *real*. Yet come the morning, he reverted right back to form.

Later that same day, when her lessons were done, Lillie found herself out of sorts. She took herself off for a wander out in the tidy rows of the wintering vines, letting the relative warmth of the Algarve sun fall all over her though she felt as dark as if she was back in Aberdeen, with a gloomy sun that started sinking near enough to three in the afternoon this time of year.

When she was not normally given to brooding.

"We need to decorate the house for Christmas," she announced when she returned, tracking dirt into his office and slouching down as far she could go in that chair.

She chose not to notice that he was obviously trying to ignore her.

"If you don't mind," he said in glacial tones, and oh, wasn't he at his most cutting today. That was how she would have known that last night was something different. Something that had stripped them both bare down to the bones, even if she hadn't already felt that way herself. "Much as I enjoy your interruptions, I do have a significant amount of work to get done."

"This can't work, you know," she said. She hadn't meant to. But the words came out anyway and she was glad of it when he didn't even do her the scan courtesy of *glancing up.*

"I'm not in the mood for histrionics today," he replied with that same frigid disinterest. "And in any case, as I have told you more than once already, there are no divorces in my family. It is not who we are."

"I'd like to know exactly who you think *we* are, actually," she threw back at him, a different kind of lightning firing up her blood. "I hear a lot about *us.* But you only ever seem to be speaking about yourself."

Tiago did look up then, though he took his time with it. Lillie thought he had a lot of nerve to bring up *histrionics* when he made such a meal out of a mere glance. "There will be no divorce, Lillie."

"I wasn't asking for one, though I'll be sure to keep in mind that you've decreed it can't occur when the time comes." She shook her head at him, as if she despaired of him. When he was like this, it was possible she did. "I mean *this* can't work. You act-ing distant and remote by the light of day and then, at night, behaving as if we are lovers in the midst of a mad, passionate affair."

"This is not the time or place for this discussion."

"Isn't it? I'm so sorry. What would be the correct time and place?" He wasn't the only one who could throw a little pageant while doing an ordinary task. Lillie quite theatrically pulled out her mobile, swiped it over to the calendar, and then waited there, poised to type in the appointment time of his choice.

She had never seen the man grind his teeth, but she thought he was close just then. "I told you. There are certain boundaries that need to be observed and it is a point of deep self-recrimination that I cannot seem to hold myself to these standards with you."

Lillie dropped her mobile to her lap. "I have an alternate idea. You could stop trying to live your life, and certainly stop trying to run your marriage, according to the whims of people who aren't even here, and didn't like each other when they were."

Maybe she shouldn't have said that. But she couldn't bring herself to take it back.

"They liked each other fine," he replied, and she wondered if it cost him to sound so emotionless. So cold, straight through. "One of the reasons they held each other in the utmost respect for all of their days is because they adhered to very simple rules. They did not attempt intimacy. It was not expected or desired. Not once I was born."

And she had already opened her mouth to argue about that. To point out to him that, fair enough, it seemed that his parents had made the best of the kind of dynastic marriage that was likely never entered into with any hope of love or true intimacy or even friendship. Liking each other, respecting each other, must seem like a triumph. A victory for the ages. She could concede that much, even if she and Tiago were something else entirely—

But instead, she stopped dead at that last thing he said.

"Is that how you're getting around it?" she asked softly. "You can excuse all these nights away because the baby isn't born yet? You can beat yourself up, but not too hard, because you haven't broken *all* the rules. Not really. But once the baby is born, that's it, I'm cut off. Is that what you're doing, Tiago?"

And she watched, fascinated, as a muscle clenched in his marvelously chiseled jaw. On another man, it would have been the same as a fist through a wall. A table overturned.

She had to repress a shudder, as if he'd done both.

"You came here to ask me about Christmas," he said, the coldest she'd ever seen him. But she knew better. She could feel the emotions he did not wish to show her, too big and too raw, crowding out the breath inside her body. "Portugal is not like your northern countries. We celebrate on Christmas Eve, but not in the manner you might be expecting. It is quiet. Restrained. Traditional. We prefer to err on the side of quiet sophistication rather than too much gaudy noise and decoration."

Every word an icicle, designed to stab her straight through the heart.

"Tiago…" she began. She tried to keep going, but her throat felt tight. Almost too tight to bear.

"If you will excuse me," he said, in that same way, whole winters in his voice, "there are calls I must make."

He did not look up again, dismissing her that easily. That completely. And Lillie staggered a bit as she left his office, from the weight of all that raw pain of his.

It was inside her now, whether she liked it or not.

And it sat heavy on all the fear and panic she'd been fighting off for too long now. Because she could see the future now, and it was the one she'd been afraid of all the while.

She kept going until she was in that central courtyard, where flowers still bloomed even now. Birds sang as if no one had told them it was December. If she closed her eyes it might as well have been the height of summer, green and lush.

"Almost as if your grandmother never agreed to forgo of all the gaudy light and color you think is so beneath you," she muttered under her breath, but out loud the same. Scowling down fiercely at bright purple and pink and orange flowers, but seeing only Tiago's frozen expression. Hearing only his frigid words.

Feeling those icicles like knives, cutting deep.

Leaving her reeling. Bleeding. Carved into chilly little pieces.

She sat down heavily on one of the stone benches near a small fountain that burbled and sang. If she closed her eyes, she could imagine it was her very own Christmas carol.

And Lillie always had loved a good Christmas carol.

When she opened her eyes again, the sun was on her face, and it couldn't have been less Christmassy if it tried.

And Lillie thought, at last, that it was high time she fought.

That she harnessed all those passions she'd been looking for all her life, and dived straight into them, for a change.

Because nothing good had come to her from waiting. Or wondering.

Or hoping he might see the light all around him.

It was high time she showed him.

As Tiago kept informing her, and not only when he was being fierce and cold from behind a desk, she was a Villela.

And if she was tracking all of her lessons, one

thing was clear in all the stories they told her. All the history on both sides of his family. Not to mention her own proud Scottish heritage.

When in doubt, they all did exactly as they pleased and sorted out reactions later. It might as well be the family motto. She reckoned she might have it sewn up and put on a fancy bit of tartan while she was at it.

Lillie took a deep breath, then blew it out, hoping any leftover icicles went with it.

But then she got up and marched back into the house to find Leonor.

Because she intended to fight with everything she had to the future she imagined, not the one he was threatening her with.

And she was going to start by having the Christmas she wanted, whether Tiago liked it or not.

CHAPTER NINE

THE FIRST HINT Tiago had that things had gone horribly awry in this home that was meant to be his sanctuary was when he left his office late a few days later, then stopped dead in the hall outside.

Because he could hear singing.

And for a tense moment he actually wondered if he was hearing ghosts, after all—

But with the next breath, reality returned, and he was more concerned that he was having some kind of a medical event, because ghosts weren't real. Not even his.

Still, the singing continued.

Tiago followed the sound from his wing of the house into the main section, not sure if he was relieved or more irritated when it became clear that he was not, in fact, imagining things. There were choirs singing.

And what they were singing was Christmas carols.

But that was not the worst of it, he discovered as

he stopped dead in his front hall and stared around in amazement. The house—*his* house, the ancestral home of his mother's people—had been transformed.

And while he had not exactly locked himself away in his office, Tiago knew he had been less available these last few days. While it was true that he had a lot of work to do, as ever, it was also true that he'd found himself a bit more keen to do it than usual.

Even after he'd realized that he was waiting for her to turn up for her afternoon tea break, which had infuriated him. What had infuriated him even more was that she hadn't, as if he'd finally succeeded in chasing her away.

This is what you want, he'd told himself sternly. *You can take this opportunity to create more space between the two of you, as you know you must.*

But he had gone to her that night anyway.

And since she'd skipped dinner, he'd had to go looking for her. He had found her back in her guest suite, which had outraged him. He had expressed that outrage by crawling into the guest room bed with her, using the four posters to great advantage as he exercised his opinion on his wife's skipping of meals and sleeping alone.

I had no idea you felt so strongly about it, she'd said, her smile sleepy and her blue eyes full of heat and laughter. *I had no idea you were* allowed *to feel strongly about anything, in fact.*

He had ignored that. Virtuously. Though he had

expressed the feelings he most certainly did not have in other, more creative ways.

But the next night, when he had to hunt her down again, he carried her across the house to his quarters because she was his wife and she should be in his bed.

A point he made certain to belabor until the dawn.

And that was the order he had given this very morning, to move all of her things into his rooms, where she belonged.

He had thought that settled it.

But instead, Lillie had turned his house into a Christmas card.

A very particular sort of Christmas card, traditional and certainly not Portuguese.

There were evergreen trees everywhere, strung with lights. And where there weren't trees, there were even more lights. There was mistletoe. There were seeming truckloads of ornaments. There was the usual nativity scene his grandmother had put up every year, mercifully left alone, but everything else was red and green, as if Santa Claus had come and exploded everywhere.

Even his grandmother's garden was not spared. There were lights strung from the surrounding rooftops, covering the courtyard in a latticework of gleaming white lights that sparkled as he glared at them.

He stood there for much too long, something simmering in him that he could not identify, but it was big. Unwieldy.

And he was not at all sure what to do with it.

Tiago turned and saw the housekeeper standing there, looking as self-contained as ever.

"Where is she?" he gritted out.

But Leonor had never been cowed by a member of his family, which was why she had stayed here so long. "If you mean Senhora Villela, she is waiting for you to join her." She did not raise her brows at him. She would not dare. All the same, the suggestion that she might remained. "I assume that is where you were headed."

"I know my way around my own house, I think," he bit out, cold. Frigid, even.

The older woman did not appear to notice the chill. "The *senhora* has prepared something special." And this time, she actually did indulge in something a little too close to a lift of her brow. "It is Christmas Eve, after all."

She did not wait for him to respond to her, because she was impertinent. And clearly did not fear that he might fire her, which, naturally, he would never do.

And in any case, he followed her. Unwillingly, or so he told himself. But he also knew that Lillie was waiting wherever it was his housekeeper was taking him, so there was no possibility, ever, that he wouldn't go.

That realization only made him…icier.

And his mood did not improve as Leonor led him outside onto one of the far patios. Where he did not find the seating areas he expected, usually quietly arranged to take in views across the vineyards that ended where the sky met the sea far off in the distance. Tonight the patio itself was transformed.

Into what he could only call…a full-on Christmas assault.

Complete with an avenue of evergreen trees, bristling with silver bells and lights, down which he was compelled to walk until he found himself in what might once have been a tastefully done seating area with braziers for a touch of heat. Now it, too, was unrecognizable and was…

"It's a Christmas grotto," came Lillie's voice, full of that deep amusement that still drove him mad. Maybe even more so today. "Isn't it magical?"

"A 'Christmas grotto'?" he repeated, as if she'd cast aspersions on his family name with that term. In truth, it felt as if she had done more than that.

"More properly, it would be Santa's grotto." She said that as if she hadn't heard his tone. As if she couldn't see—with her very own eyes that were as blue as the sky and never before the slightest bit blind—how he stood here before her, clearly in no way transported by these shenanigans.

He ordered himself to keep that steadily growing sense of unease at bay. That growing unwieldiness that seemed to make the very ground beneath his feet buckle and shift when he knew full well that every-thing on these lands had been built to withstand the march of generations.

But he also took the opportunity to take a good, hard look at his wife.

The wife of Tiago Villela, mother of the future Villela heir, was dressed in bright red and green as if she imagined herself a holiday elf. Instead of what she actually was—one of the wealthiest women in the world.

He made a mental note to restrict both colors from her wardrobe in future.

The dress she wore looked like velvet and was therefore completely inappropriate for the Portu-guese climate, even on a night like tonight when the weather was relatively cool. As if that was not enough, she wore a pair of knee-high boots in an overbright red leather. He supposed the heels on those boots added length to her already well-formed legs, and no doubt to her height as well. He estimated that would put her red-slicked mouth in a fascinating place before his, but he could only imagine it because she was not standing before him.

She was *lounging*. On what looked like one of those ghastly peppermint candy canes that were fes-tooned about everywhere Christmas was not con-tained, when the rational part of his mind understood that she had simply transformed a settee with red and white fabric.

Tiago was opposed to holidays of any sort and liked Christmas least of all, because it had once been his grandmother's favorite. He didn't like to think about how much she had loved it, and how he had, too, while she'd been alive. It was far better to simply hate it, ignore it, and move on. But it was hard not to think that he might as well rethink his historic dislike of the season if the packaging was like this. Making his ripe, lovely wife look like a Christmas sweet herself.

She had made the whole of this part of the long, wide patio into a Christmas scene, lifted from a climate far north of here. All those evergreens festooned with lights. Some kind of cottony fluff strewn about to replicate snow. Tiago had never personally experienced such a Christmas, but he had seen it. Like everyone else alive, he had been subjected to cold-weather Christmas images the whole of his life.

But tonight it was simply one step too far.

"This is unacceptable," he told her grimly.

Lillie shifted position on her candy-striped settee, but only slightly. As she did, the dress moved and he found himself distracted by the way the hemline rose, showing him the creamy expanse of one thigh.

He gritted his teeth.

"Merry Christmas Eve to you, too," she said, sounding lazy and merry at once.

"First of all," he said, not sure why he felt half-drunk when he hadn't touched alcohol. Not tonight.

Though he thought a shot or two of the hard stuff would not go amiss as he faced down this outrageous temptation. "You are in Portugal. Everything you've done to this house seems to suggest that you are confused. Geographically."

"What I am," Lillie replied, a quiet note in her voice that was at odds with all the surrounding commotion, "is married to a man who does not communicate with me. If you are opposed to Christmas, you should have said so."

He did not like the way she said that. *Opposed to Christmas.* As if *he* was the issue here. "I'm not opposed to Christmas. What I am opposed to is my family's ancestral home being turned upside down with all these tawdry and tasteless decorations."

"Why don't you like Christmas?" she asked, calmly, as if he hadn't just questioned her taste, the infernal woman.

"I don't like Christmas or dislike Christmas," he told her impatiently, though he was aware this was not as true as it could have been. Still, it was what he wished to believe. What he'd long assured himself he believed. "I never believed in fat men in red suits tallying up my misdeeds to see whether or not I might receive a gift. My parents held the typical *consoada* on Christmas Eve, as is tradition. We went to church because that's what one does. On Christmas we ate turkey, lamb, and goat when I was small. But after my grandmother died, the rest of us merely ignored the holiday entirely. She was the one who insisted on a proper Christmas meal. We were just as happy to forgo that once she was gone."

He wasn't sure what he expected after that simple statement of fact, but it wasn't the way Lillie looked at him then, her blue eyes suddenly too bright for his liking. "Tiago. That's terribly sad. You do know that, don't you?"

That massive *thing* inside him shifted again, making him doubt he could trust himself to stand and he could not allow that. He would not.

"I understand that you have an emotional connection to the holiday," he said stiffly. "But that does not mean everyone must. Perhaps I should have foreseen that you would react in this way, as you are so far away from your home and no doubt experiencing a great many physical and—"

But he stopped when Lillie laughed. In that airy, entertaining manner that he wished he hated. That would make it easier. He ought to find her embarrassing, surely, but he didn't. That was the trouble. She was like clear, sweet air and he wanted to inhale her and—

Focus, he ordered himself.

"If you're about to comment on my hormones, there's no need. I've always loved Christmas. I've always decorated for it, too." She shifted on the settee, somehow drawing that hem up even higher, yet still *barely* preserving any shred of modesty, and he felt himself come perilously close to breaking out in a sweat. He rather thought she knew it. "And for all the lessons you seem determined that I should take on board, here's one for you. It's only a few decorations. Perhaps on a grand scale to match the house we're in. But Tiago. I promise you that it's not going to hurt you any to ignore them, if you must."

And she stayed where she was, *lounging* at him and too delectable by half, and how was he supposed to handle her when she was so outside the boundaries of everything he knew, everything he'd been taught?

Tiago didn't know what to do with her. That was the trouble.

He gazed down at her, and as ever, there were too many warring impulses fighting for purchase inside him.

Did he want to go to her? Sprawl there beside her? Get his hands on that lush body of hers and put his mouth where he wanted it most?

Or did he think that it was far better to indulge only the reality of this, which was that he knew how their marriage ought to be run. He knew exactly what needed to be done to make certain that his family legacy was preserved.

He could not understand—and had not been able to understand, at all, since the moment he had laid eyes on this woman—why it was that she seemed to muddy waters he'd long believed were crystal clear, all the way down.

When he knew where that mud took him. Back to grieving in the dirt and cut off for his trouble.

Tiago had vowed he would never let him drown like that again.

"I think there are some things that need to be clarified between us," he said, aware that his voice was harsh.

But even as his words hung there in the air, his staff began to flood in, bearing platter after platter and piling them high onto the table that waited on one side of the red and green and snowy seating area. The table, too, was gleaming with gold and silvers, bright glossy reds and exuberant greens.

Lillie rose to her feet for the food, clapping her hands together before her like a child. Except she was no child, he recognized. She was unbearably earnest, and she had never been taught to hide her enthusiasm for any reason, and there was nothing in the whole of him, his entire personality and experience, that had the slightest idea what to do with that.

Or with her.

As he had demonstrated since she'd walked into his office in London.

Though he found he liked the idea that she was even less guarded than she'd been then. That she'd been honest, but wary. And he wasn't sure he knew exactly when she'd decided to be this open, this gloriously transparent.

Only that it had happened here, with him.

And that he had come to hunger for it.

"I worked with the kitchens on the menu," Lillie told him, clearly delighted with all of this. "It's a proper Scottish Christmas dinner. Roast turkey and all the trimmings. Cranachan, clootie dumpling, Dundee cake, and proper mince pies for sweets. We have Christmas carols playing, fake snow on the ground, and finally, a little Christmas cheer round here."

She smiled at the servants as they passed her on their way out of the little evergreen cave she'd made them, then turned that meltingly bright smile on him, so vivid that it outdid all the lights she'd strung up.

And she made him ache, that was the thing. She pierced him straight through the heart, when he had gone out of his way to make sure that organ held no sway over him. Ever.

Because the only purpose of the heart, as far as he could tell, was to hurt.

Tiago had no time for such things.

He let the heel of his palm press against the offending spot on his chest, hard, and then he glowered at the woman who had caused this in the first place. With all that infernal *brightness*. Those blue eyes that would be the undoing of any man. And that laughter that he worried would haunt him through the rest of his days.

"I don't want any of this," he said, his voice so dark that there was a part of him that was shocked it didn't put out all her twinkling lights.

Her smile dimmed as she straightened where she stood. "I'm sorry to hear that."

"If I wanted a British Christmas, I would go back to London. I don't need it foisted upon me here."

He thought she looked at him too long, then. And he was afraid she saw too much.

As she had from the beginning.

"But you see, I will need my child not only to be fluent in your languages and able to eat with the proper utensils when called, but to be familiar with the things that are important to me, too," she said. "I think that's what making a family is all about, isn't it?"

And there was something about how calm she sounded that only pricked at him more. Because why should she be calm? How *dared* she? Tiago was known for his glacial composure and unshakeable calm with everyone on the planet, save her.

Why should he be the one to feel as if the earth was shaking beneath him when she looked as if she could stand just as she was, forever?

That ungainly thing inside him seemed to grow with every breath, crowding out everything else. Making him wonder if he had never really known the true contours of who he was at all.

And that, too, he had to lay squarely at her feet.

"If I am permitted a moment of honesty, Lillie," he growled out then, as dark and as harsh as he liked. "The unvarnished truth is that you are entirely inappropriate."

"Inappropriate?"

He had expected her to flinch at that, and hated himself that he wanted this to happen, but it couldn't be helped. Surely the truth was what was important here. It needed to be said at last, and he had never before worried about being the one unafraid to voice even the most unpleasant of truths.

Though it didn't seem as if she'd truly heard him, because all she did was raise a careless sort of brow.

"I went to a meeting in Spain and it somehow ended up ruining my life," he continued, darker and harsher. "I don't know how it happened."

"Don't you?" She sounded...bland. Much too bland. "I remember exactly how it happened. And I'm not sure I believe that you can't."

"Never in my life have I taken leave of my senses the way I did that night." He shook his head as if it was a horror, the memories that came at him. When the only horror was that those memories claimed as much of him as they did. Even now, when he should have had his fill of her by now. He should have moved on and he hadn't. He couldn't. He didn't understand why. "All this time later, I still can't make the slightest bit of sense of it."

"It's a terrible mystery," she said, as if she was agreeing.

But the way she folded her arms above her round

belly indicated that she was not agreeing with him at all.

"I have spent my entire life being raised for one thing," he told her, perhaps too intensely. "My destiny has never been in doubt. There is no argument to be had, no wiggle room. I was brought into this world to carry on my family's legacy and to uphold to the best of my ability all the duties and responsibilities that are part of that." When she started to open her mouth, he shook his head to stop her. "Part of what has always been expected of me is an excellent marriage. It was expected—*demanded*—that I would find an heiress to an exceptional line. A woman of spotless lineage, whose family legacy would complement my own."

"It sounds a bit like you're discussing breeding a horse."

"Because, in a way, I am." He knew he was not making his case in the cool, considered manner he preferred. But he needed her to understand him, at last. He more than needed it. He thought that if she didn't, he would have to begin to consider unthinkable options. Like the divorces Villelas did not indulge in.

Because they didn't have to, he understood now. Because none of his ancestors had made such a terrible choice in a wife.

"You're comparing this to horse breeding?" she

asked, but that laugh of hers raked over him as if she had taken a razor to his skin.

"We do not come from the same place," he said, severely. "That is simply a statement of fact. It was never my intention to marry for any reason at all save the perpetuation of my family line. From the time I was very young, I knew full well that I was never to allow chemistry or emotion to be my guide. And do you not see why? Do you not see the trouble we are already in?"

"If we're in trouble," she said, and he didn't like the way she was looking at him. Too carefully, to his mind. As if she was trying to figure out how best to *manage* him. As if he *required management*. "And I'm not saying that I think we are. But Tiago—if we are, don't you think that has rather more to do with the fact that you can't seem to decide who you are?"

She could not have said anything to offend him more. To strike more deeply into the places he held most sacred inside him.

For a moment he felt winded.

But then a kind of storm rushed in, a fury all its own. "I know exactly who I am. There has never been a moment I drew breath where I was not keenly aware of my *precise* position in this world."

"In the world, perhaps. But not in this house." And she pressed her lips together for a moment, though he couldn't have said if it was to keep words in or simply because her frustration was that great. *Her* frustration. "You are one man when the sun goes down, Tiago. Raw. Passionate. A man who smiles and sometimes even laughs. Most of all you're fully present. And then, every morning, the sun rises and that man disappears. And in his place is a creature of stone and distance, like some kind of gargoyle."

"You have that backward," he grated out, too far gone even to take offense at being compared to hideous statues. "This gargoyle you speak of? He is who I really am. It is the other man who is the aberration. And it will stop now. I should never have let this happen in the first place."

"But you did let it happen." She took a step toward him, shimmering red and green and her hair curling wildly around her head. "You let it happen, when, as you have been at great pains to tell me, you have been the master of the universe, or at least *your* universe, since the day you were born. Surely the fact that you did not stop it the way you said you were going to—that you, in fact, clearly enjoy our nights together as much as I do—suggests that you've got this wrong."

"The only thing I have gotten wrong," he told her, his voice like steel slicing through wood, "is in imagining that I could take such a lump of clay and fashion it into a proper Villela wife. It is a Herculean task and it turns out, even I am no demigod after all."

She blinked at that, but once more, she didn't quail. Instead, Lillie raised her chin again, and the sheer

bravery of that gesture made something in him…
howl. Despite his efforts to shut it down, it kept on
and on, like too much grief to bear.

"I may not be the perfectly sourced work of art
you were expecting to marry," she said after a moment in a voice he couldn't read, her gaze darker than
before. "But who wants to live out their lives with an
actual oil painting? I prefer a real, live, often deeply
flawed person."

"I'm not trying to insult you," he growled at her,
though that *deeply flawed* cut at him. "I am only taking heed of the unchangeable facts of the situation."

"You mean…that I'm pregnant with your child?
Or that you're the one who insisted on marrying me
in the first place?"

He slashed his hand through the air and focused
on the facts. Because if anything could save him,
it was facts. Facts did not roar and carry on inside
him. Facts did not drape lights everywhere and talk
of *being present*. Facts were cold and unemotional,
just as he was supposed to be.

"You have no lineage worth mentioning," he
pointed out, as if ticking off items on that list he'd
mentioned long ago. "You have no fortune—in fact,
I believe you have precious little money at all. Nor
were you a properly raised, untouched virgin when
we met, raised to give herself over to her husband
and his bloodline for all eternity."

"You, of course, were as pure as the driven snow."

She said that dryly. And again, he couldn't see any hint of hurt, or awareness, or any of the things he would have expected her to feel. She looked neither wounded nor shamed nor remotely impressed with her own unsuitability.

He hated himself for laying it all out so baldly, so rudely, but this was reality, wasn't it? And he was tired deep into his bones of being the only one who seemed to be even remotely aware of it.

"The sad truth is that the only thing we have in common is a troubling physical connection that in and of itself should have excluded you from consideration in the first place," he said, forcing himself to finish this when he should have had this very conversation that day in London. Before he'd found that memories of her were pale imitations of the real thing. "It is nothing but the wildest, most unhinged folly to imagine that we will ever find common ground. This Christmas scene you have created only underscores these facts."

"I don't know what makes you think that just because you have all the money in the world you get to control your heart, Tiago," Lillie said softly. "No one else can."

"I can," he threw back at her. He felt something raw surge inside of him, sharp-edged and engulfing, like desperation. But he was a Villela. And Villelas did not do *raw* or *desperate*. They did not. "I have to, Lillie. This is not a negotiation."

"Fair enough," she said. "That's quite a list. It's no wonder you don't have a queue wrapping round the place."

And then, far from bursting into tears, running off, or any of the responses he might have expected from her, she only shrugged.

As if…she didn't care?

Why did that make all those raw places in him… worse?

But in the next moment she made it even more precarious by smiling. And not that bright, earnest, Christmas light of a smile she'd aimed at him already tonight.

This smile he recognized.

Because he usually saw it when they were in bed, and she was astride him, rocking herself against him, hard, for the express purpose of tearing him into pieces.

It was that wicked. It was that knowing.

Keeping her eyes fastened to his, she reached down and took the edge of her dress in her fingers, then began to tug it up.

Tiago meant to tell her to stop. He meant to insist that she cease and desist right this very moment. But he couldn't seem to get the words out of his mouth.

And so, as he stood there as if frozen into place by forces outside his control—which was exactly how everything had felt with this woman from the start— she pulled her dress over her head and tossed it aside.

Leaving him dry-mouthed and too taut, everywhere, at the discovery that she wore nothing at all beneath it.

Lillie was standing there wearing nothing at all but those bright red boots, that riot of curly dark blond hair, and their baby.

She looked ripe and perfect.

And he might not have cared much for Christmas, but there was no denying that the way the lights danced over her skin was a kind of blessing. She looked rosy, bright.

Lit from within.

Tiago couldn't seem to do anything but stand there, as incapable of movement as if someone had come and struck him on the head, and then she made it worse by smiling at him all over again because she was wicked to the core.

Because she had been a sorceress from the start.

"I meant what I said," he managed to get out.

"And I heard you." But that smile only deepened, and there was pure fire in the blue of her siren's eyes. "Pity you can't resist me, isn't it?"

CHAPTER TEN

LILLIE HAD NEVER seen a man…break apart while standing still.

And she never would have imagined that Tiago could—that he would allow that loss of control.

But as she stood there, wearing nothing but her boots and the conviction she carried deep in her bones that she knew what was happening here even if he didn't, she watched him…crumble.

A look very much like anguish made his face twist. And for a moment she thought she'd miscalculated and made a terrible mistake. That this was something else entirely from what she'd assumed it was—

But even as that thought formed in her head, he was moving toward her. He was reaching out with those clever hands of his and that anguished look in his blue-green eyes turned instead to a storm she knew well.

She not only knew it. She longed for it.

Tiago lifted her up and swung her into his arms, as he did so often. And he held her there for a long moment, so intense that she felt suspended somewhere between the lights in the trees and the storm in his gaze. She was aware of the way his chest moved, harsh with every breath, as if somewhere, somehow, he was running flat out when she could see he was standing still.

"You are a sorceress," he growled with his head bent to hers. In a voice nearly too dark to bear, with all that thunder laced through it.

She lifted her hand and put it to the side of his face, where she could feel that muscle clench, once and then again.

"It's not my magic," she whispered. "It's ours. The only difference is, I'm not afraid of it."

The sound Tiago made then, raw and wild, thrilled her. So too did that sudden blaze of something not quite fury in his gaze.

And then everything went white hot and molten.

He took her down onto that chaise she had made into its own ornament. And he came with her, his hands frantic on his clothes, until he could press against her, skin to skin.

At last, she thought, as if it had been an eternity since last they'd touched instead of a matter of hours.

Then Lillie stopped thinking altogether.

Because it really was magic, this thing between them. It was an enduring glory, what he could make her feel with a single touch. And she was nothing but wildly, deeply, eternally thankful that he did so much more than simply touch her.

And better yet, that she could practice that same magic right back at him.

So that if there was a sorcery, shimmering there between them on this Christmas Eve, it belonged to them both.

It was the way he took her breasts in his hands, as if they were precious, making her nipples sing and the rest of her clench on a wave of that delirious pleasure. It was the way she crawled over him and then down the length of his body, so she could kneel between his legs and take that satiny length of him, hot and heavy, in her fist.

Then, better still, bend her head to taste him.

If it was magic, then spell after spell, they made it better. Deeper. More perfectly theirs.

They spun it out into the sweet sea breeze and the smell of pine, chasing that storm as it spiraled deep inside each of them and then bloomed hot and sweet.

Once, then again.

Because once was never enough.

And when they were finished, when they both lay there, panting and limp with the beauty of it all, there were so many things that Lillie wanted to say to him. The words crowded on her tongue.

But before she could get even one of them out, he moved. Not far.

Tiago rolled so he sat at the edge of the candy cane settee. He propped his elbows on his knees, and put his head in his hands. She sat up, too, not liking the look of that for this proud, beautiful man—

In the next breath, he straightened, raking his hair back from his face.

But he still did not look at her, and Lillie thought she knew why. Because there was not a hint of that iceman who had stood before her earlier, sharing that list of all her deficiencies. Enumerating all the ways she would never live up to whatever ideal he had in his head of who his wife should be.

And therefore how he would never live up to the people who'd put those ideals there in the first place.

"You want me to be nothing more than a husk of a man, broken beyond repair," he said, in a low voice she hardly recognized as his. "And I do not understand why."

Lillie had the urge to laugh at that, but she didn't. And was glad she didn't in the next moment, because there was no way he would take to that lightly. It didn't matter what she thought was happening here. What mattered was that he was experiencing it as brokenness.

And she believed that he felt that way. It was just that she suspected that the thing that bothered him was the *feeling* part. Not what might or what not be broken in him because of those feelings.

She reached over and carefully, gently, smoothed

a hand down his back. He reacted instantly. He stiffened, then sighed.

And still did not look at her, almost as if he didn't dare.

"I don't want you broken, Tiago," she said quietly. She pulled in a breath, then let it go, and since this was a night for the telling of truths, decided it was time she told him the only truth that could matter. "Don't you know? I love you. And what I want is you *alive*. In every possible way."

But she knew even before the words were all out that she'd gone too far. Because he was moving then. Tiago stood, that graceful, athletically masculine body somehow jerky tonight. As if he was stiff with some particular arthritis that only all these Christmas lights and unsanctioned *feelings* could give him.

And when he turned to look down at her, he looked betrayed.

"What did you say to me?"

"That I want you fully alive," she replied at once. "Not simply going through the motions. Not ticking off boxes on a list that someone long dead made up to make sense of their own unhappiness. That's not living. That's simply existing, and I—"

"You love me?" he interrupted her to demand, still looking and sounding as if she'd stabbed him through the heart.

This time, she did let out a laugh, mostly because she was startled.

"Of course I love you," she said, baffled. "How could you imagine otherwise?" Now it was her turn to rub a hand over her face. "You're not the only one who doesn't normally trot off with a stranger at a Spanish resort. I've certainly never done anything like that before, and didn't intend to do it again even before I found out I was pregnant. I didn't believe in love at first sight before you, but I certainly do now." She shrugged helplessly. "Obviously."

And she had not intended to say all of that, she supposed. She might have had the odd fight with phantom versions of Tiago in a mirror or two, but she wasn't unaware of the state of her relationship with this man. It was one thing in the night. But that was *only* in the night.

There was daytime Tiago to contend with and she didn't need a primer on the fact he wouldn't be receptive.

Though it was possible, she could admit as he stared at her in an amazement that she found a touch insulting, that it was sheer stubbornness that made her say it now.

And also because it was true. She didn't see why she should pretend not to know the truth of things just because that truth might upset him. It wasn't as if he'd held himself back from sharing his thoughts on how she fell short.

"No," Tiago said, what felt like several lifetimes

later, all of it caught in that gaze of his the way she always was.

And he did not elaborate.

He simply said the one word, flatly. Coolly. As devoid of emotion as if he was discussing bloody office supplies, she rather thought.

Lillie blinked, but he only stared back at her. No longer did he have that look of betrayal on his face. No hint of that anguish from before. It was as if he was wearing a solid stone mask of Tiago Villela. As if he was one of the statues that littered his grounds.

She understood at once that this was what he wanted. This was exactly who he was trained to be. And this was what he had been telling her all along—that this was all he ever wanted to offer anyone.

But she refused to accept that.

"It wasn't a yes-or-no question," she said, keeping her voice as careful and quiet as she could though her heart was pounding wildly in her chest. "It was a statement of fact."

Tiago's eyes gleamed, but darkly. "What it was, Lillie, was the last straw."

And the way her pulse was careening about began to seem like more of an alarm, but she found that she was frozen in place. She could do nothing but watch him as if through a glass wall as he moved around the candy-cane-colored settee, gathering up his things. He hauled his trousers up over his hips. He threw his shirt on, but did not button it.

"These delusions cannot be indulged," he said when he'd accomplished those things, in that same flat way. "It is already a disaster. What we must do is perform the necessary triage, now."

"I'm sorry, I'm not following. What are the delusions?"

But he ignored her. Then she watched as this man who reacted so little raked his hand through his hair again, seemingly unaware that he was doing it. He made a noise that she rather thought would have been a full shout from another man, but from him was little more than a growl. "It's not your fault. It's mine. I should have followed my instincts and known that there was no possible way that you could understand."

"I am many things," Lillie said, feeling a spark of her temper ignite—something that came as a relief after all the raw emotion and biting back the things she wanted to shout at him like the fishmonger's wife he clearly thought she was. "A grubby peasant cluttering up the hallowed halls of the Villela family, clearly. Unworthy of the great honor of having been knocked up by you, anonymously. Message received. But I've never been an idiot, Tiago. I understand with perfect clarity what's happening between us."

"Evidently you do not."

She went still because she had never heard him raise his voice before. It made her heart knock hard against her ribs, and not because she was afraid.

And he continued, getting louder as he went. "Clearly you have no comprehension of what you've done. I told you. I keep trying to tell you. What you're talking about is the antithesis of everything I have done and everything I have left to do. I don't believe in love, Lillie. I can't. I won't."

She cleared her throat because it felt tight. "None of those are the same thing," she pointed out.

He moved then and a sudden, wild surge of joy rippled through her, because she thought he was going to put his hands on her again—

But he did not.

Sadly enough, all he did was scoop her dress up off the ground and thrust it toward her.

Lillie took it and held it to her, though she did not put it on.

"The duties and responsibilities that are mine to handle cannot be clouded by emotion," he ranted at her. His eyes blazed. His mouth was twisted, and he slashed his hand through the air again, and harder this time. "There is no possibility that any good can come of pretending otherwise. It was a mistake from the start to allow this—to let our physical connection take hold. I blame myself."

"As far as I can tell, you blame yourself for everything," Lillie said as blandly as she could when her heart had moved to her throat. "Even when no blame is required."

"Because you don't understand what's at stake," he threw at her. "How could you?"

"Here's a news flash, Tiago. There's more to the world than spreadsheets, bank balances, and endless talk of family legacies."

"You make light of the situation because you're not suited to it," he bit out. "This is why, I understand now, my parents were so determined that I understand how crucial it was to marry within my class."

And Lillie might have been offended by that—maybe she ought to have been—but she wasn't. Mostly because she knew exactly who she was and where she came from, and she wasn't the slightest bit ashamed of it.

But she also didn't think he was *trying* to offend her. The man was simply stating the facts as he knew them.

So she swung her legs over the side of her candy cane couch, and stood. And she did not pull her dress on over her body as he obviously wished she would, because she wasn't a saint here. She was no more and no less than a woman in love, fighting for something she'd never expected to find in the first place.

She was, at last, the woman her parents had raised her to be.

Finally, she had found something worth fighting for.

And she was stubborn, wasn't she, because she did not intend to let go of it.

Whether he believed in it or not.

"Your mother and father sound like miserable people to me," she said, careful to keep any emotion from her voice, then, because otherwise she reckoned he would hear only the feelings, not the words. "It seems as if they married in cold blood and barely tolerated each other, then decided that those things were virtues. And who am I to question what works for someone else? But you're not them, Tiago."

"I know I'm not," he threw back at her, still loud in ways the glacial Villela heir never was. Ever. "Because if I was either one of them, I never would have allowed this to happen. I never would have let it get so bad."

"And if you hadn't," she threw right back at him, "we wouldn't be expecting this baby. And I can't regret the fact that we are. Even if I'd never found you again, I have every intention of loving this child for as long as I live. I already do."

"You can love whatever you like," he thundered at her then, his face in the grip of all those things he didn't believe in. "But I will thank you to leave me out of it. I will be the appropriate father to my heir. I will teach this child what is expected. What is necessary. I will not traffic in these childish notions of yours. Christmas grottos. Santa Claus. *Love.*"

He spat those things out as if saying them might take him out at the knees, especially that last.

"Believing in magic doesn't make you weak," Lillie said softly, with her whole heart, because he had all the wealth and consequence in the world, but she had that. And she'd bet on her heart any day. "It isn't something that's inflicted upon you—it's a gift. It's only people who can't believe in themselves who struggle with it. Because what is magic but another word for love, Tiago? And it isn't weak people who love. It's the strong. The brave." When he looked as if he might argue, she shook her head. "You already know this. Because every night, we strip each other bare. Until we are both raw, vulnerable, naked in every sense of the word. If it wasn't hard, if it wasn't *terrifying*, you wouldn't have to hide from it in the light of day."

He didn't like that. She saw him reject it, even as a different sort of storm worked over him. "I'm not hiding from anything. I'm trying to break the spell I should never have allowed to take hold of me in the first place. Because there are certain responsibilities that need to be met, Lillie. Like it or not. And if you can't concentrate on those responsibilities, we will have to make certain that we find you an environment where you can focus on what's actually important."

She didn't like the sound of that, but she didn't let herself pay attention to the way her stomach dropped, or the worry that swept over her. She didn't let herself tip over into the fear of what she thought he was threatening. Because he wasn't talking about only her when he talked like this.

And she couldn't bring her child into the family he kept describing. She wouldn't.

Lillie stepped forward then, heedless of her nudity, and pointed a finger in his face. And she could see by the arrogant astonishment in the way he reared back that no one had ever done anything like it before.

"Let me tell you what my responsibilities are," she threw at him, no longer caring if he heard her voice shake. "They do not involve worrying over much about a family name. They have nothing to do with your houses. Or chilly dinners where we act as if selecting the correct fork is the only thing that stands between us and a barbarian horde at the gate."

"You have no idea—" he began.

But she only jabbed that finger at him again, as if she might thump him in the next moment, and she was as surprised as he looked that he fell silent.

"My responsibilities are to love the man that I married, as best as I'm able, and cherish this baby we made together. No more and no less." She pulled in a breath. "And you are not the only person on the planet who takes his responsibilities seriously."

And for a long moment, they both stood there, bathed in twinkling Christmas lights. Christmas carols swept all around them from the strategically placed speakers, all sounding like choirs of mourning to her now. Perfectly harmonized grief, only highlighting and underscoring how unhinged the both of them were while they belted these things at each other that smarter people might know better than to say.

She could see it in him, in the way his hair was disheveled for the first time since she'd met him, his eyes so dark, and his chest like a bellows.

Lillie didn't think she was in any better state.

He stared back at her, once again looking as if she'd delivered him a mortal wound. He took a step back. And another, and stopped only when it looked as if he might crash straight into a Christmas tree.

"Tiago…" she whispered.

"No, *benzinho*," he said, a gruff sound of anguish this time. *"No."*

Then he turned and pushed his way through the trees, setting off in the direction of the vineyards. Out into that rolling, lovely land that stretched out from this house and reached to the sea. All of it his.

All of it a prison.

And Lillie wanted to run after him. She wanted to *fight*. She wanted to *do something*, whatever she could and however she could.

But she couldn't make him love her if he didn't.

Maybe, she thought, just maybe—she'd been horribly wrong about all of this from the start.

Lillie pulled her dress on over her head then. It fell into place and she pushed her curls back out of her face.

And there, surrounded by the bright glare of the

Christmas lights while choirs sang softly of days merry and bright, she wrapped her arms around herself, and cried.

Because for the first time since she'd found out that she was pregnant with Tiago's baby, Lillie felt truly alone.

CHAPTER ELEVEN

TIAGO STAGGERED FROM the patio, down the stairs, and didn't realize he had neglected to put his shoes on until his bare feet hit the earth.

He couldn't remember the last time he had allowed himself to go barefoot, and certainly not here in the dirt. Not here on this land of his, of his family, that had defined him for the whole of his life—both here and in Spain, where the Villela stronghold was far less pastoral.

A true steward of the land would indulge in it more, he thought. And he had the sudden memory of his grandmother kneeling in her garden, looking at him with her wise green eyes.

Dirt is medicine and water is magic, and a wise man knows how to use them both in their time, meu dengo, she had told him.

He hadn't permitted himself such memories since he was small. And tonight, he felt neither medicine nor magic. What he felt instead was the coldness of the earth beneath his feet. Not frozen, for this was still the south of Portugal. Not frigid or too hard.

But certainly it felt dark and cold here, so far away from the woman who smiled at him, pointed fingers at him, and wrecked him by asking him to do the one thing could not.

He could not. He would not.

Tiago started forward, his usually cool and rational brain whirling around in a haze.

It wasn't only that he felt like a stranger to himself, loud and unruly and unsteady on his own feet, but now the world seemed to feel strange around him. When whatever else he had felt, he had always been certain that he belonged right where he was.

He accepted that it was possible, as only Lillie had ever dared say, that his parents might have been miserable people. But that hadn't mattered, not when what they had in common was this.

The family. The legacy.

These lands and what they meant, throughout time.

He didn't know how he was meant to lose that, too—that connection to history and the future that had sustained him all his life—and his first reaction was a bright-hot fury at Lillie for holding up a mirror he never wanted to look into.

Tiago, who had always prized his own steadiness, staggered on a while longer, but then stopped again.

Because suddenly the cold dirt beneath his feet, the careless stars overhead—it all seemed futile.

Because where could he go?

If there was a place on this earth where Lillie would not haunt him, wouldn't he have found it by now?

Despite himself, despite all the promises he kept making to himself, he found himself turning back.

And then he was looking back at the house. He saw all the light, beaming out into the dark like beacons. The lights he expected to see and all the Christmas fervor Lillie had brought to this place.

All that bright and unapologetic light, and all of it reminded him of her.

The way her blue eyes lit up when she saw him. The way she smiled, heedless and wide open. That laugh of hers, infectious and bawdy and so necessary to him now that Tiago could not comprehend how he truly believed there was any way to survive without it.

No matter how he tried to castigate himself for his weakness, it remained. As stubborn as she was. As rowdy as those irrepressible curls of hers.

He let his gaze find that patio she'd taken over with that silly grotto of hers, all red and green and foolish.

It wasn't as if his opinion on it changed, but it looked different from out here in the dark. It looked like a bright and happy bit of folly, a touch of the frozen north here, where it never snowed—except perhaps in the mountains at Monchique.

And for the first time, he wondered if it was possible that Lillie was a little bit homesick for all that cold, damp, and all-day gray.

He found himself raking his hands through his hair once more and as he did, his gaze kept moving—

Until he found her.

And his heart seemed to seize inside his chest.

Because in all the time he had known her, Tiago had seen this woman in a thousand intimate ways. In bed and out. When his doctors visited to check on the baby. At her lessons, at the table—she inhabited all the roles he threw in her with that same laugh and her careless ease, because no matter her pedigree, she possessed the confidence of a queen.

But tonight she stood on the edge of the patio, looking out into the dark.

Tiago doubted she could see him, but he could see her. Far too clearly. Because he could see the way she slumped a bit as she stood. How she wiped at her cheeks, then hugged herself again.

Because Lillie, *his Lillie*, was crying.

And he had told her that he was broken before. But he knew now that he hadn't even started.

Because watching her cry was the end of him.

Everything he'd said to her, everything Tiago had believed the whole of his life—none of that held a candle to what rushed through him at the sight of this woman in pain. Weeping, because of him.

What he said. Who he was. Because of everything, perhaps.

He found himself moving again as if she'd called him to her.

And there was a part of him that wished she had, because he could have ignored it, then. He could have used it as more evidence that everything about her was wrong—that everything he'd said to her was true.

For a moment there, he tried to convince himself—

Instead, she wiped at her cheeks again and her face crumpled, and everything in him simply…ended.

And then began again.

With the breath that moved him toward her. With each step that brought him near, because the land that owned him was useless if all he could do when he stood upon it was hurt her.

Tiago took the stairs two at a time and finally found himself walking toward her, his hands already outstretched, to touch her. To hold her. To simply be near her.

As if she had been the candle in the window all along.

"Why are you crying?" he demanded, and that wasn't what he meant to say at all. Not so harshly. So gruffly.

Lillie offered him a tremulous smile, so unlike

the one he was used to, and he reached out to wipe another tear away.

"I was waiting for you," she said, her voice thick. "I didn't want you to get lost."

"*Benzinho*, how can I get lost?" He did not drop his hand from her face, though his voice was urgent and gruff and he was sure he would not recognize himself if he looked for a reflection. "I grew up here. I know every inch of this land, backwards and forwards."

"It's not the land I'm worried about," she said quietly. "It's your poor heart, Tiago."

He kept breaking. He kept breaking and breaking when he should have been too broken to crack apart any further.

For a moment he did not know if he could speak again, but then he did. "My grandmother did not only tend flowers," he told her, keeping his gaze on her face. On her overbright blue eyes that showed him the only version of himself he needed to see. "She also took care with me, her only grandchild, because she said she did not like how stiff my parents were. Her Christmases were filled with light, like yours. She sang songs every day on the way to the Epiphany, and there were sweets to make the singing better. *Bolo Rei* and *Bolo Rainha* cakes to tempt anyone. Every kind of fried, breaded thing you can imagine. And always at least one *lampreia de ovos*. She was a disciplined woman in her way, but not when it came to Christmas."

"Because Christmas is no time for discipline, Tiago," Lillie said with mock severity. "Magic requires comfort food. Everyone knows that."

There was no reason his throat should feel as tight as it did then. "When she died, my mother wasted no time in ridding the house of all the things that brought my grandmother, and me, that joy. She told me it was childish. That she, too, had enjoyed such things as a foolish child, but she had grown up." He watched her intently, desperate for her to understand. Or maybe it was that he wished to understand himself, with every word he said. "Over time, I began to see even the hint of happiness as the same kind of thing. Childish. Embarrassing, because joy and light were for fools. And one thing I could never be, with all the responsibilities that waited for me, was a fool."

"Tiago," she began, but her voice cracked, so he did, too.

"I never saw you coming," he blurted out, the words too gruff to keep to himself. "I'm ashamed to say I would have run from you if I had. I never wanted this, Lillie. I wanted to stay as I was, wrapped up tight in the armor I've worn almost all my life, secure in the knowledge that nothing and no one could ever affect me. I learned, year after frigid year, how to make sure I loved nothing. My parents taught me well. They did not love each other or anything else. They did not love me. I told myself I had no need of such nonsense. That it had been the immature longings of a child that I had ever imagined otherwise, and I had outgrown it. I had come to think myself invulnerable. And then there you were."

"I don't know," she whispered, her lips curving again. "Maybe it was the sangria after all."

"I kept making boundaries and then breaking them myself," Tiago said in that same rough way, as if this kind of honesty hurt, so raw and real. No ice involved. "I thought if I pushed you away by day, it could erase what happened in the night. But it never did."

"Nothing could erase you," she said softly. "Nothing ever did."

"And despite all the things I did to you, so desperate to keep you at a distance, to make you pay for the things I did not wish to feel, here you are." He shook his head, all those cracks inside him filling, then, with wonder. With her. Siren blue eyes and all that bright light, even in the dark. "Standing before me, worrying about the state of my heart."

"The thing about hearts," Lillie said with as much sternness as she could muster, "is that they beat whether you want them to or not. And they keep on beating no matter how sternly you tell them to stop. And I'm afraid that that's what love is like as well,

Tiago. It doesn't give you choices. It just allows you opportunities. If you dare."

Tiago did the only thing that felt right, then. He swept her up in his arms and held her there, his face close to hers. He looked deep into her fathomless gaze, losing and finding himself there the way he had since that very first moment.

He saw her tears, her fierce determination, so much of her light—and saw, too, her hope.

So much hope, and nothing could have humbled him more.

He shifted her, setting her down so that she leaned back against the balustrade. Then he stood there before her, letting his hands frame her lovely face. Then tracing patterns down her sweet neck, along her arms wrapped in soft velvet.

He smoothed his palms over that firm, round belly where his child grew.

"I'm not sure I believe that I have a heart," he told her in a low voice, a confession he would make to her only. "But I have no need of it. Because our baby's heart beats right here." He leaned down and pressed his lips to her belly, feeling more than hearing the little sob she let out. Then he straightened, settling his hand in that sweet space between her breasts. "And your heart beats here. And I have to believe that I will learn enough to find my own, in time. If you let me try."

"I love you," she whispered. "And I already know where your heart is, Tiago. I always have."

"I would have told you that I could never love." But he gathered her close, and she melted into his arms. "Yet since the moment I laid eyes on you, I have never been without you. In those five months when you were lost to me, I carried you inside me. And just like now, every night, you wanted me. While I was asleep. While I was awake. Every night, I woke with your taste on my lips. Back then I wished I knew your name. Now I do, and it is like a song in me."

"I love you too," she said, and as he watched—though her cheeks were still damp and her eyes were too bright—she gifted him with that smile.

That big, beautiful, wide smile that felt like laughter inside him and made him feel that he belonged in a way that land never could.

He understood, now. All he had to do was love her, and he would always fit. All he needed was her, the family they made, and he would never be cold again.

For a man who had always believed himself impervious to the vagaries of weather, Tiago understood then that all he'd wanted, all his life, was warmth.

Light. Joy.

All those things he had locked away.

As if all along, he'd been waiting for the key.

For a woman with a siren's eyes and chaotic hair to upend all his preconceptions and bring him home.

"You will have to teach me, *minha vida*," he said.

My life, he'd called her, and she was. He leaned down to kiss her on the forehead, the tip of her nose so that she laughed, and then, finally on her mouth. Like a vow.

"I want to live like you do. So brave. So open. I want to learn how to love as you do, beyond all reason."

She tipped her head back and slid her hands up along his chest, making him realize he had been walking around with his shirt wide open, which was something he would never have dreamed of doing before. And now he couldn't imagine why.

He was Tiago Villela, was he not? He could do as he pleased. And he thought it was about time he started.

Especially when he watched his wife, his Lillie, light up there before him, and then laugh as if she'd known how this would be all along. The two of them like this, their baby on the way, and nothing but choirs singing in between them.

"I'll tell you right now," Lillie told him when the laughter danced away into the pine trees standing tall around them this Christmas Eve. "It's as easy and as hard as this. All you do is look for the light and the joy no matter how it scares you. And hold on to me, just like this." She reached down and took his hands in hers, lacing their fingers together. "And then we'll do it together."

And they did.

Starting right then and there, bright all the way through.

CHAPTER TWELVE

FIVE YEARS LATER, Lillie spent Christmas Eve morning dressing herself in a beautiful white gown. She had her mother at her side, tearing up at the slightest provocation and fussing with all the flowers the staff had cut from the courtyard garden.

And when it was time, she gripped her father's arm as he walked her down the aisle they'd made that led to the fountain in the center of the garden, where even on the twenty-fourth day of December, the sun shone down like a blessing.

Today of all days, Lillie thought, that's exactly what it was.

"We're so proud of you, my darling girl," her father said roughly as they walked. And Lillie grinned up at him, so hard it made her face hurt.

All of her friends from university sat waiting for her and across the aisle, the friends Tiago really did have sat with matching smiles. Because Lillie and Tiago had spent these years strengthening their bonds in all kinds of relationships, not only with each other. Even Patricia, her old boss, was here, happily sporting her latest Spanish tan and a lover to go with it.

Tiago had flown with her to Aberdeen before the new year began. And Lillie had taken far more pleasure than she should have when she'd brought him into that shared house that had been her home for so long, that he had reacted to as if it was an actual prison cell she'd only narrowly escaped.

She packed up her things and then left without looking back.

Because, finally, she knew her purpose. Her life had meaning because she loved, was loved in turn, and had a child on the way. Those three simple facts changed everything. Infused everything. Made sense of everything.

Tiago and her parents circled each other a bit warily at first. But when it became clear that everyone involved loved Lillie to distraction, they found their way to a friendship that was grudging at first, and then bloomed into its own kind of beauty.

Lillie moved down the aisle, happy that once she'd left Aberdeen behind, she'd found her way back to herself. To the woman who fought for what she wanted, wasn't afraid to stand up for herself, and let herself get vulnerable. She and Tiago had spent a lot of time learning how to love each other, something that only worked when they both let themselves love fully and wholly.

Once it had been clear that Lillie also had a head for finance and business, Tiago had wasted no time giving her access to the company too, so that she couldn't have been bored if she tried.

Though every now and again she claimed she was, just to see what her ferociously inventive husband would do.

Her father stopped at the head of the aisle and kissed her on the cheek, then solemnly handed her over to the best man.

The best little man there ever could be, Lillie thought as she gazed down at sturdy little four-year-old João with eyes like a stormy sea, and a mess of dark curls.

"Come, *Mãe*," the Villela heir, who was normally a mischievous bolt of light and energy, told her sternly. "It's time to get married."

Lillie looked over at Leonor, who held one-year-old Carolina in her lap, named for the great-grandmother whose gardens bloomed around them even now. The baby gurgled happily and waved her chubby fists.

And Lillie let her son lead her forward, to where Tiago waited for her.

Tiago, who had dedicated himself to the task of learning how to love with all of his considerable strength and power.

And now the man known as a glacier left his iciness at the office.

At home, he laughed and sometimes, like the night when Carolina had come too fast into this world and they had thought they might lose her, he cried.

But he never let go of Lillie's hand. He never stopped searching out that light, that joy.

And he never stopped relying on the heart that Lillie had found in him when he'd thought he'd somehow lived his whole life without one.

"Lillie," he said now, "*você é tudo para mim*. You are everything to me. Light of my life, at last."

The night before he had made her sign papers all over again, though she had laughed at him and told him he was being silly. Something he could not have heard five years ago, but found entertaining these days. These papers, to the horror of his entire legal team, invalidated all that had gone before.

"You're in for it now," she told him when she signed. "I can divorce you at any time and take you for everything you're worth."

"You do that every night, my love," he replied.

And they had practiced, there in the study, to be sure.

Now, his hand wrapped around hers and he pulled her to him. To stand there with him so they might renew their vows and have the wedding they'd hurried through the first time around.

Though they knew, even if no one else did, that

the truth of the matter is that their fate had been sealed by the side of a pool in Spain. At a resort that Lillie insisted they visit at least once a year, even though she now knew how little Tiago cared for the place.

What does it matter? she always teased him. *You like the bed just fine.*

I like you, he always replied. *It doesn't matter where.*

Though he was still aristocratic enough to complain, every time.

They stood there in the courtyard where his grandmother had taught him how to love, long before his parents had encased him in ice. And finally, they said all of those things out loud that had always been there between them.

Right from that very first glance that had knocked them both sideways.

With the weight of all the things they were to each other, immediately, even when they were strangers.

They spoke of love, and light. Of the children who were little terrors, and utter joys, and who would be welcoming another sibling in the spring.

They spoke of trust, of medicine and magic.

And when it was time to kiss his bride again, Tiago swept Lillie up into his arms, kissed her thoroughly, and then carried her down the aisle.

Later that evening, they celebrated Christmas Eve in the Portuguese style, there in that rambling old house where her children believed in the possibility of Santa Claus, and their four-year-old could barely sleep among all those Christmas trees and candy cane settees, and the lights on all the trees seemed brighter every year.

"But I know the truth," Tiago said as he moved in her long after midnight, while their children and their guests slept. "The magic is in Christmas, *minha vida*. It's you. It's always been you."

"It's love," she whispered back. "And it's ours."

"Forever," Tiago agreed.

And as they lost themselves in this lightning-bolt dance of theirs, old and familiar and new every time, Lillie found herself laughing.

Because she knew that forever was only the beginning.

Love was like that.

And true love was even better.

* * * * *

Did you fall in love with
A Billion-Dollar Heir for Christmas?
Then make sure to check out these other
Caitlin Crews stories!

The Accidental Accardi Heir
A Secret Heir to Secure His Throne
What Her Sicilian Husband Desires
The Desert King's Kidnapped Virgin
The Spaniard's Last-Minute Wife

Available now!

#4161 BOUND BY HER BABY REVELATION
Hot Winter Escapes
by Cathy Williams

Kaya's late mentor was like a second mother to her. So Kaya's astounded to learn she won't inherit her home—her mentor's secret son will. Tycoon Leo plans to sell the property and return to his world. But soon their impalpable desire leaves them forever bound by the consequence...

#4162 AN HEIR MADE IN HAWAII
Hot Winter Escapes
by Emmy Grayson

Nicholas Lassard never planned to be a father. But when business negotiations with Anika Pierce lead to his penthouse, she's left with bombshell news. He vows to give his child the upbringing he never had, but before that, he must admit that their connection runs far deeper than their passion...

#4163 CLAIMED BY THE CROWN PRINCE
Hot Winter Escapes
by Abby Green

Fleeing an arranged marriage to a king is easy for Princess Laia—remaining hidden is harder! When his brother, Crown Prince Dax, tracks her down, she strands them on a private island. Laia's unprepared for their chemistry, and ten days alone in paradise makes it impossible to avoid temptation!

#4164 ONE FORBIDDEN NIGHT IN PARADISE
Hot Winter Escapes
by Louise Fuller

House-sitting an idyllic beachside villa gives Jemima Friday the solitude she craves after a gut-wrenching betrayal. So when she runs into charismatic stranger Chase, their instant heat is a complication she doesn't need! Until they share a night of unrivaled pleasure on his lavish yacht, and it changes *everything*...

#4165 A NINE-MONTH DEAL WITH HER HUSBAND
Hot Winter Escapes
by Joss Wood
Millie Piper's on-paper marriage to CEO Benedikt Jónsson gave her ownership over her life and her billion-dollar inheritance. Now Millie wants a baby, so it's only right that she asks Ben for a divorce first. She doesn't expect her shocking attraction to her convenient husband! Dare she propose that *Ben* father her child?

#4166 SNOWBOUND WITH THE IRRESISTIBLE SICILIAN
Hot Winter Escapes
by Maya Blake
Shy Giada Parker can't believe she agreed to take her überconfident twin's place in securing work with ruthless Alessio Montaldi. Until a blizzard strands her in Alessio's opulent Swiss chalet and steeling her body against his magnetic gaze becomes Giada's hardest challenge yet!

#4167 UNDOING HIS INNOCENT ENEMY
Hot Winter Escapes
by Heidi Rice
Wildlife photographer Cara prizes her independence as the only way to avoid risky emotional entanglements. Until a storm traps her in reclusive billionaire Logan's luxurious lodge, and there's nowhere to hide from their sexual tension! Logan's everything Cara shouldn't want but he's all she craves...

#4168 IN BED WITH HER BILLIONAIRE BODYGUARD
Hot Winter Escapes
by Pippa Roscoe
Visiting an Austrian ski resort is the first step in Hope Harcourt's plan to take back her family's luxury empire. Having the gorgeous security magnate Luca Calvino follow her every move, protecting her from her unscrupulous rivals, isn't! Especially when their forbidden relationship begins to cross a line...

YOU CAN FIND MORE INFORMATION ON UPCOMING HARLEQUIN TITLES, FREE EXCERPTS AND MORE AT HARLEQUIN.COM.

HPCNMRB1123

HARLEQUIN
PLUS

Try the best multimedia subscription service for romance readers like you!

Read, Watch and Play.

Experience the easiest way to get the romance content you crave.

Start your **FREE TRIAL** at
<u>www.harlequinplus.com/freetrial</u>.